TWENTY MINUTES FROM ROME

A play for television

by

FRANCIS DURBRIDGE

WILLIAMS AND WHITING

Cover design by
Timo Schroeder

9781912582556

Williams & Whiting (Publishers)

15 Chestnut Grove, Hurstpierpoint,

West Sussex, BN6 9SS

Titles by Francis Durbridge published by Williams & Whiting

Murder At The Weekend – the rediscovered newspaper serials and short stories

Also published by Williams & Whiting:
Francis Durbridge : The Complete Guide
By Melvyn Barnes

Titles by Francis Durbridge to be published by Williams & Whiting

My Friend Charles
One Man To Another – a novel
Paul Temple and the Alex Affair
Paul Temple and the Canterbury Case (film script)
Paul Temple and the Conrad Case
Paul Temple and the Geneva Mystery
Paul Temple and the Gilbert Case
Paul Temple and the Gregory Affair
Paul Temple and the Jonathan Mystery
Paul Temple and the Lawrence Affair
Paul Temple and the Madison Mystery
Paul Temple and the Margo Mystery
Paul Temple and the Spencer Affair
Paul Temple and the Sullivan Mystery
Paul Temple and the Vandyke Affair
Paul Temple Intervenes
Portrait of Alison
Step In The Dark
The Desperate People
The Doll
The Other Man
The World of Tim Frazer
Three Plays for Radio Volume 2
Tim Frazer and the Salinger Affair
Tim Frazer and the Mellin Forrest Mystery
Two Paul Temple Plays for Radio
Two Paul Temple Plays for Television

INTRODUCTION

Francis Durbridge (1912-98) was from 1933 a prolific contributor to BBC Radio of plays, sketches and musical libretti. But 1938 saw him carve his name in the niche that made him one of radio's biggest names, when his serial *Send for Paul Temple* was so popular that it launched a succession of Paul Temple serials lasting until 1968. These serials also proved successful overseas, with translations using European radio actors in at least ten countries.

Then from 1952, while continuing to write for radio, Durbridge turned to television. He later explained this in an interview (*Radio Times*, 21 October 1971): "Twenty years ago in the United States, a producer told me that I was wasting my time by not going into television. So that's what I did – I tried to build up a reputation with serials, since I'd vowed never to write a Paul Temple episode for television." The result was that *The Broken Horseshoe* (1952) entered the record books as the first thriller serial on British television.

While Paul Temple remained a radio detective, Durbridge became a trademark for television thrillers that teased with red herrings, cliff-hanger endings to each episode and the certainty that no character should be believed whatever they might say. This parallel reputation for television serials saw protagonists struggling in webs spun by killers who remained concealed until exposed in the final episode, and as with his radio serials Durbridge conquered Europe with numerous television productions in at least six countries until the 1980s.

Throughout the 1950s and 1960s UK television viewers were mesmerised by Durbridge's ingenuity, with *The Broken Horseshoe* (1952) quickly followed the same year by *Operation Diplomat* and then *The Teckman Biography* (1953), *Portrait of Alison* (1955) and *My Friend Charles*

(1956). He then continued to write television serials until 1980, with an awesome appeal. A review of *The Scarf* (*The Times*, 10 February 1959) commented: "When he writes a script nowadays Mr. Francis Durbridge takes full advantage of his position as undisputed master of the detective serial. Boldly stamped across the screen, his signature is less the mark of an author than a brand name, guaranteeing the quality of the goods." And when a new production of *Melissa* was televised, Stanley Reynolds (*The Times*, 12 December 1974) wrote: "He is plainly and simply a master of mystery … And here it is where the men are separated from the boys, and Mr. Durbridge from the mundane writers of 'tecs and thrillers … It has a nightmare quality, a touch of the Franz Kafkas – no wonder Durbridge is a great favourite on German telly."

Such was Durbridge's success on television that for all his serials from 1960, beginning with *The World of Tim Frazer*, the BBC gave him the unprecedented accolade of the "*Francis Durbridge Presents*" screen credit before the title sequence of each episode. And in 2006, in an obituary of the Professor Quatermass creator Nigel Kneale (*The Independent*, 2 November 2006), Jack Adrian stated that: "During the 1950s and 1960s Nigel Kneale bestrode the world of British television like a colossus (and) the only writer who came anywhere near him in terms of sheer entertainment and popularity was Francis Durbridge."

But Durbridge eventually re-considered his decision to exclude Paul Temple from television, and as *The Stage and Television Today* reported (6 November 1969): "Among new series are *Paul Temple*, the detective created by Francis Durbridge, who comes to television for the first time with Francis Matthews in the title role." And Durbridge himself, in the *Radio Times* (20 November 1969), said: "I wanted to hold off putting Temple on television, because I wanted to establish myself as a television writer quite apart from the character of Temple. And having done that – I'd had many offers for Paul Temple from various sources – I felt now was the time to put him on."

So from 23 November 1969 Francis Matthews and Ros Drinkwater appeared in four series totalling fifty-two episodes until 1 September 1971, and for these television films some thirty writers provided original screenplays with Durbridge prominently credited as the creator. But although he did not himself write any of the televised episodes, three synopses that he wrote have recently been discovered – *Murder in Advance* (a new version of his 1960 newspaper serial *Deadline for Harry*); *The Elusive Miss Helvin* (a new version of his 1955 magazine serial *The Man Who Beat The Panel*); and *The Calcary Case*. In fact *The Calcary Case* was the only one taken up, adapted by screenwriter Paul Erickson as *Re-Take*, episode 13 in the second series, 26 July 1970.

It must be confessed, however, that we know little about the recently discovered television script *Twenty Minutes from Rome*, except that it was never screened and almost certainly written long before the Paul Temple television series. There are a few clues that date it as mid-1950s, quite early in Durbridge's television career, and we can link it with the fact that in 1954 – following the success of his first three television serials – it was reported that he had written a one-off play for television. Indeed the *Yorkshire Post* (8 September 1954), previewing the autumn BBC television season, mentioned that "Plays include a specially commissioned thriller by Francis Durbridge". And what is more, Durbridge's financial ledger on 24 June 1954 recorded the receipt of a half fee in advance for a "single 90-minute television play" – so an educated guess might easily arrive at *Twenty Minutes from Rome*.

At the very least, there is now an unprecedented opportunity to read the previously unknown television script

Twenty Minutes from Rome. Some might consider it a typical example of the sort of plot that made Durbridge's name, while others might dismiss it as lightweight when compared with his gripping television serials. But either way, its publication today represents a further piece added to the fascinating Francis Durbridge jigsaw.

Melvyn Barnes
Author of Francis Durbridge: The Complete Guide (Williams & Whiting, 2018)

PRINCIPAL CHARACTERS:

Geoffrey Ryder
Alan Quinton
Detective Inspector Mann
Colonel Smith
Walter Smedley
Ronald Freed
Katherine Weldon
David Weldon
Stella
Sergeant Gorringe
Dr Charles Elroyd
Harold Bolton
Mr Henson
Dr Stevens
Dr Ross
Waiters, Telephone Operators,
Nurses, A Business Man, Porter,
Airport Official, Hotel Receptionist

OPEN TO: The face of a large ultra-modern clock.

The small hand is stationary at 12 o'clock. The minute hand moves slowly round the dial until it reaches twenty minutes to the hour, then it stops. The moment the minute hand stops the numeral "12" disappears and the word "Rome" takes its place.

CUT TO: A House in Whitehall. ALAN QUINTON's Private Study.

This is a large room, tastefully, if somewhat richly, furnished.

ALAN QUINTON is sitting at the desk reading a report: there are several telephones on the desk, a morning newspaper, folders, half a dozen leather bound notebooks, and a cigarette box and lighter. QUINTON is a man of about fifty; good looking in a rather scholarly way. He has a dry sense of humour.

The door opens and a pleasant young man called RONALD FREED enters and crosses to the desk.

FREED: We've just received a cable, sir. He arrived safely; everything went according to plan.

QUINTON: (*Nodding*) Good.

FREED: (*Smiling*) I expect you're very pleased it's all over, sir.

QUINTON looks at the young man and slowly puts down the report he is reading.

QUINTON: I beg your pardon?

FREED: (*Nervously; realising that he has said the wrong thing*) I said – I expect you're very pleased it's all over, sir.

A moment.

QUINTON: How long have you been in my department, Freed?

FREED: About six months, sir.

3

QUINTON:	Well, when you've been with me a year, you'll realise I'm hardly ever pleased about anything.
FREED:	Yes, sir.
QUINTON:	I'm sometimes relieved, occasionally amused, and frequently exasperated – but never pleased.
FREED:	I understand, sir.
QUINTON:	(*With a nod and faint smile*) I'm relieved to hear it. I've been hearing extraordinary reports about your work just recently, Freed. They tell me you cracked the Swiss cipher.
FREED:	(*A shade embarrassed*) Yes, sir.
QUINTON:	How long did it take you?
FREED:	Four hours …
QUINTON:	(*Pleasantly surprised*) Four hours!
FREED:	Well – three hours and forty-eight minutes to be precise, sir.
QUINTON:	You timed yourself?

FREED nods.

QUINTON:	You must have felt confident! … Three hours and – ?
FREED:	… Forty-eight minutes, sir.
QUINTON:	(*Impressed*) M'm … (*Nods; dismissing FREED*) Very well, I'll see the Inspector.
FREED:	And Mr Ryder, sir?
QUINTON:	(*Picking up the newspaper*) Yes, and Mr Ryder.

FREED goes out.

QUINTON looks at the newspaper for a moment, then puts it down on the desk and gathers up the various notebooks; he locks the books in a drawer and is replacing the key in his waistcoat pocket when DETECTIVE INSPECTOR MANN and GEOFFREY RYDER enter.

4

The INSPECTOR is an educated man in his late fifties. He wears a lounge suit and carries a soft hat. GEOFFREY RYDER might be any age between thirty-seven and forty-five. He is normally a good-looking man but at the moment his features appear drawn and tired; his manner is slightly tense. QUINTON rises and shakes hands with the INSPECTOR.

QUINTON: Inspector …

MANN: Good afternoon, sir. This is Mr Ryder.

QUINTON: (*Shaking hands with GEOFFREY*) Ah, yes! (*Indicating the newspaper on his desk*) I've just been looking at your photograph, Mr Ryder. (*He looks down at the paper*) It's not a very good one.

GEOFFREY: I'm afraid I'm not very photogenic these days.

QUINTON looks up at GEOFFREY; he is not quite sure how to take this remark.

QUINTON: Yes, well – sit down, gentlemen. (*He sits at the desk. GEOFFREY and the INSPECTOR facing him. He nods to the cigarette box*) Help yourself to cigarettes.

MANN: Not for me, sir – thank you.

GEOFFREY hesitates, then he leans forward and helps himself to a cigarette from the box. QUINTON picks up the desk lighter and offers him a light; they study each other for a moment.

QUINTON: (*Putting down the lighter*) Well, Inspector, what can I do for you?

MANN: (*A shade uneasy*) I don't know that you can do anything for me, sir. But – (*He looks at GEOFFREY*) as you already know, Mr Ryder is a witness …

GEOFFREY: (*Correcting MANN*) Suspect, Inspector …

MANN: (*Turning towards GEOFFREY; irritated*) Very well, sir – suspect, if you prefer the

5

word. (*To QUINTON*) Mr Ryder is a suspect in a very important murder case, but he's refused to make a statement to me, the Assistant Commissioner, or anyone else at Scotland Yard.

QUINTON: Well?

MANN: Well, for some obscure reason he's quite prepared to make a statement to you, sir. At least, he says he is.

QUINTON looks at the INSPECTOR, then across at GEOFFREY.

QUINTON: Why to me? I'm not connected with the C.I.D., you know. I'm a Civil Servant; head of a Government Department.

GEOFFREY: Do Civil Servants usually have offices like this – in Whitehall?

QUINTON: (*With the suggestion of a smile*) The photogenic ones, Mr Ryder. (*He picks up a ruler from the desk*) But you haven't told me who mentioned my name in the first place?

GEOFFREY: (*After a moment's hesitation*) Dr Elroyd.

QUINTON: (*Examining the ruler*) Dr Charles Elroyd?

GEOFFREY: Yes.

QUINTON: (*Looking up*) When did you see Dr Elroyd?

GEOFFREY: About three weeks ago.

QUINTON: Where?

GEOFFREY: In London.

A moment.

QUINTON: (*Quietly*) Go on …

GEOFFREY: Dr Elroyd said that you were head of a department responsible for screening government personnel. He said that if I wanted a job at Stanfield, I should have to

6

	submit myself to a personal investigation by your department.
QUINTON:	That's true. But why should he tell you that?
GEOFFREY:	I wanted to work at Stanfield. I applied to Dr Elroyd for a job.
QUINTON:	Are you a scientist?
GEOFFREY:	No, I'm a metallurgical chemist, specialising in powder metallurgy. That's why I wanted to work at Stanfield.
QUINTON:	(*Thoughtfully*) I see. (*He looks at GEOFFREY for a moment*) Mr Ryder, forgive me, but you don't look at all well – have you been ill recently?
GEOFFREY:	Yes. I've been in hospital.
QUINTON:	Oh, I'm sorry. Which hospital were you in?
GEOFFREY:	The one for tropical diseases in Great Paddington Street. You see, I suffer from malaria and about five weeks ago I was suddenly … (*He hesitates*)
QUINTON:	Yes, go on …

GEOFFREY rises and crosses to the desk; he stands for a moment, tense, undecided, then he stubs his cigarette out in the ashtray and turns towards Quinton.

GEOFFREY:	Mr Quinton, do you mind if I start this story at the very beginning? If I don't you won't understand why I came here this afternoon, why I – particularly wanted to see you …
QUINTON:	(*Nodding*) Go ahead, Mr Ryder. Start your story at the beginning.

GEOFFREY still hesitates, then crosses to his chair and sits down facing QUINTON.

GEOFFREY:	My name is Geoffrey Ryder. I am a New Zealander by birth although I've lived most of my life in this country and on the Gold Coast

7

of West Africa. I am a bachelor, and I am forty-two years of age. I qualified as a metallurgical chemist in February '45 and in August of the same year I started work for a Liverpool firm, called Stanley Brighouse. I was with Brighouse for six months and then I landed a job with the West African Chemical Company; their headquarters was on the Gold Coast, and I was stationed there from March 1946 until September of this year. I sailed for England on the S.S. Uganda on September 4th. It was my intention to come straight through to London when the boat refuelled at Cherbourg but I decided, more or less on the spur of the moment, to spend a few days in Paris. I arrived in Paris on September 26th.

QUINTON: Go on, Mr Ryder.

GEOFFREY: I'm afraid Paris was a disappointment. It rained for the first two days, and I found, much to my astonishment, that the food didn't agree with me. Also, strange though it may seem, I was very lonely. On my last night in Paris, I visited a night club called La Drap D'Or. It was a large, expensive place just off the Champs Elysee.

FADE IN: Background of Dance Music.

FADE IN: The flashing neon sign advertising the entrance of La Drap D'Or.

GEOFFREY's VOICE: I hadn't reserved a table, so I stood at the bar most of the time drinking champagne and watching the cabaret.

CUT TO: The crowded entrance of La Drop D'Or.

People are waiting for tables; checking hats and coats. The cabaret – a group of dancing girls – can be heard but not seen.

At a corner table, WALTER SMEDLEY is sitting alone. He is a well-built man in his middle fifties and at the moment he is a little the worse for drink. He wears a dark lounge suit. There is a small lamp on the table and an ice bucket on the floor containing two empty champagne bottles.

Waiters and guests swirl past the table and there is an atmosphere of smoke, noise, music and confusion.

People are obviously dancing near at hand, although we cannot see the main floor of the room or the dancers.

GEOFFREY's VOICE: When the cabaret finished, I noticed a man sitting at one of the tables. I'd seen him before somewhere, but I couldn't place him; then I realised that we were both staying at the same hotel and that we'd bumped into each other in the Grill Room. He was an Englishman and I discovered later that his name was Walter Smedley.

A WAITER stops at the table and puts a plate down with SMEDLEY's bill on it then goes. SMEDLEY picks up the bill and glances at it. He puts it down; after a moment he picks it up again and stares it.

SMEDLEY: (*Looking for the WAITER*) Garcon! Garcon, come here a moment. (*He has a slight North Country accent*)

The WAITER reappears.

WAITER: Monsieur?

SMEDLEY: (*Tapping the bill*) What do you call this?

WAITER: L'addition, monsieur.

SMEDLEY: L'addition!

9

WAITER:	Oui, monsieur.
SMEDLEY:	I should think it is l'addition. Eleven thousand eight hundred francs …?
WAITER:	Oui, monsieur!
SMEDLEY:	(*Offering the WAITER the bill*) Well, take it away and do a bit of subtraction!
WAITER:	(*Ignoring the plate*) No, no, monsieur … (*Referring to the bill*) Two bottles of champagne, one chicken sandwich … cigarettes … service … eleven thousand eight hundred …
SMEDLEY:	Now wait a minute! Wait a minute! Not so fast … What do you mean, two bottles of champagne?
WAITER:	(*Perplexed*) Two bottles, monsieur.
SMEDLEY:	Don't be stupid! I haven't had two bottles. I couldn't drink two bottles. I'd go pop!
WAITER:	(*Protesting*) But, monsieur, you ordered …
SMEDLEY:	Now look, don't argue the point, take the bill away, knock a couple of noughts off it and then bring it back, there's a good chap. (*He mops his brow*) An' while you're at it, bring me a lager …
WAITER:	I'm sorry, monsieur – (*Pointing to the bill*) but this has got to be paid …
SMEDLEY:	I know it's got to be paid, an' I'll pay it – when it's right.

LEON arrives at the table; he is a tough looking Frenchman: he wears a white dinner jacket and a gardenia.

LEON:	(*To the WAITER*) What seems to be the trouble?
WAITER:	(*A shrug*) L'addition …
SMEDLEY:	(*To LEON*) Not an unusual complaint, I imagine.

LEON:	(*Taking the bill and scrutinising it*) What do you object to, sir?
SMEDLEY:	Well, amongst other things, I object to being charged for two bottles of champagne when I've only had one.

LEON looks at the WAITER; there is a brief conversation in rapid French.

LEON:	(*To SMEDLEY*) The waiter says you have had two bottles.
SMEDLEY:	(*Annoyed*) Oh, he does!
LEON:	Yes.
SMEDLEY:	I don't care what the waiter says …
LEON:	(*Indicating the ice bucket by the side of the table*) There are two bottles here, monsieur …
SMEDLEY:	(*Surprised; looking down at the bucket*) What? Oh, so that's the game, is it? (*Picks up one of the empty bottles and looks at it*) Well, he's the rotten apple in the barrel to start with! (*He drops the bottle back into the bucket*)
LEON:	Are you suggesting that we placed an empty bottle …
SMEDLEY:	(*Getting up from the table; beginning to get very annoyed*) I'm not suggesting anything! Now, I don't want to be awkward, old chap – altho' I can be a very awkward customer if I want to be. (*Ticking off the items on his fingers*) I've had one bottle of champagne, one sandwich – we'll call it chicken for argument's sake – and one packet of cigarettes.

There is a pause.
LEON looks at SMEDLEY.

LEON:	Very well, monsieur.

LEON takes a pencil from his pocket, alters the bill, and returns it to SMEDLEY who looks at it; he is obviously surprised.

SMEDLEY: Ten thousand four hundred …?

LEON: Correct, monsieur …

SMEDLEY: You've knocked fourteen hundred francs off!

LEON nods.

SMEDLEY: So, it's ten thousand four hundred francs for a bottle of bubbly and – (*Throwing the bill down in disgust*) You must think I'm a Billy-Muggins!

LEON picks up the bill and holds it out towards SMEDLEY.

LEON: You'd better come to the office, monsieur.

SMEDLEY: (*Raising his voice*) I'm not going to an office. I'm staying right here. (*Emphatically*) And I'm not paying ten quid for a bottle of champagne and a sandwich.

LEON: (*Taking hold of SMEDLEY's arm; trying to lead him from the table*) Please, it would be better if you came to the office.

SMEDLEY: (*Releasing his arm and raising his voice even louder*) This is where I had the snack, and this is where I'm discussing it! (*He takes out his wallet*) Now, I'll tell you what I'll do. I'll pay you for the cigarettes, I'll give you six hundred francs for the sandwich, and I'll give you a couple of quid for the champagne …

At the bar, several people are staring across at SMEDLEY's table; amused by the incident. GEOFFREY is at the bar; he looks considerably less tense and very much happier than in the preceding scene with QUINTON. He is wearing a lounge suit. We can hear SMEDLEY's voice above the noise of conversation and music. GEOFFREY looks across at SMEDLEY's table.

12

SMEDLEY:	I've told you, I'm not paying ten quid for a bottle of champagne and a sandwich …
LEON:	But the cabaret, monsieur …
SMEDLEY:	I know all about the cabaret, I've seen it … An' very nice too, but there wasn't ten quid's worth … Now, you either take what I'm offering you or …

We focus on GEOFFREY. As we hear the sound of a sudden blow and SMEDLEY falls across the table, GEOFFREY's expression changes; he has seen the blow. We go back to the table and SMEDLEY is leaning across it, having apparently passed out. He is supported by LEON and the WAITER.

GEOFFREY:	(*To SMEDLEY*) Are you all right?
SMEDLEY:	(*Dazed*) I think so … (*He tries to lift his head up*) What happened? Did someone hit me?
LEON:	(*Brusquely; to GEOFFREY*) Is he a friend of yours?
GEOFFREY:	No, we happen to be staying at the same hotel, that's all.

SMEDLEY stands holding his jaw; confused and bewildered.

LEON:	Well, take him back to the hotel – please, monsieur – we don't want any trouble.
GEOFFREY:	(*To LEON*) Then it's a pity you hit him.
LEON:	(*A mechanical smile*) He fell, monsieur, and caught his head on the lamp. (*A shrug*) It was an accident …

GEOFFREY looks at LEON, then picks up SMEDLEY's wallet off the table.

GEOFFREY: How much does he owe you?

LEON nods to the WAITER, and ignoring GEOFFREY, walks away.

WAITER:	(*To GEOFFREY*) Eleven thousand eight hundred francs, monsieur …

GEOFFREY opens the wallet. The camera focuses on GEOFFREY's hand on the wallet.

CUT TO: The wallet on a table in a hotel bedroom.
The camera pans from the table to a door which leads into a bathroom; the door is ajar and there is the sound of a shower. After a moment the shower stops, and SMEDLEY emerges; he has had his head under the cold shower, and he is now drying himself with a towel. He is fully dressed, except for his jacket and tie and collar. GEOFFREY is sitting in an armchair watching SMEDLEY.

GEOFFREY: Feel better?

SMEDLEY: I feel a lot better, thanks very much …

SMEDLEY crosses and takes his tie and collar from a dressing table.

GEOFFREY: I've ordered some coffee – black coffee.

SMEDLEY: A cup of tea's more in my line … (*Grinning*) But I won't say no to a nice cup of coffee.

GEOFFREY: How's the chin?

SMEDLEY: (*A little self-conscious*) Feels all right … (*He waggles his eye*) No bones broken … My word, he packed a wallop, didn't he? If I'd known he was that tough, I'd have kept my big mouth shut.

GEOFFREY: What was the argument about – the champagne?

SMEDLEY: (*Putting on his tie and collar*) Yes, they reckoned I'd polished off a couple of bottles.

GEOFFREY: And had you?

SMEDLEY: (*Thoughtfully*) I don't know. I was certainly very muzzy.

GEOFFREY: (*Amused; pointing to SMEDLEY's wallet*) Well, I'm afraid you paid for two anyway.

14

SMEDLEY:	(*Straightening his tie*) I should have paid up at the beginning and not made such a spectacle of myself. I feel quite ashamed. (*Turning towards GEOFFREY*) By the way, the name's Smedley – Walter Smedley.
GEOFFREY:	(*Rising and shaking hands*) I'm glad to know you, Mr Smedley. I'm Geoffrey Ryder.
SMEDLEY:	Well, many thanks for what you did, Mr Ryder. I appreciate it.
GEOFFREY:	It was nothing.
SMEDLEY:	I wouldn't say that. I doubt whether I should have found my way back if it hadn't been for you. By the way, before I forget, I owe you for the taxi. (*He picks up the wallet*) How much was it?
GEOFFREY:	Oh, that's all right. I was coming back to the hotel anyway.
SMEDLEY:	Are you sure?
GEOFFREY:	Yes, of course.
SMEDLEY:	Well, that's very decent to you.
GEOFFREY:	Is this your first trip to Paris?
SMEDLEY:	No, I've been before. Used to come a lot in the old days – when the wife was alive. We used to come in the spring when the chestnut blossom was out. My goodness, it was a picture. Have you ever been here in the spring, Mr Ryder?
GEOFFREY:	Once. It rained every day.
SMEDLEY:	(*Laughing*) Go on! Well, there you are, you see …
GEOFFREY:	How long are you staying?
SMEDLEY:	Oh, I'm only passing through; I'm off to Genoa tomorrow.
GEOFFREY:	On holiday?

15

SMEDLEY:	No, no, business. I'm in the shipping line. We've just opened an office at Genoa and I'm taking over for six months.
GEOFFREY:	That should be interesting.
SMEDLEY:	I suppose so, but I'm getting a bit old for that sort of thing. (*He is patting his pockets, feeling for his cigarette case*) Besides, it means living in a hotel for six months and I can't say I'm fond of it. I've got a very nice place in London, very nice. I was sorry to leave it. (*Still feeling in his pockets*) I hope I haven't lost my cigarette case …

GEOFFREY takes out his cigarette case and offers SMEDLEY a cigarette.

GEOFFREY:	Have one of mine …
SMEDLEY:	Oh, thanks. (*He accepts a cigarette and takes a lighter from his pocket*) What's your line, Mr Ryder? Engineering? Research?
GEOFFREY:	You're not far out. I'm a metallurgical chemist.
SMEDLEY:	Really? My wife had a cousin that was a metallurgical chemist; did very well for himself too.
GEOFFREY:	I've been abroad for eight years. I'm on my way back to England.
SMEDLEY:	Spot of leave, eh?
GEOFFREY:	Not exactly …
SMEDLEY:	Well, don't tell me you're retired – not at your time of life.
GEOFFREY:	(*Smiling*) No. I've had a touch of malaria, so I thought it was about time I came home.
SMEDLEY:	Where were you – the Congo?
GEOFFREY:	No, West Africa. A place called Takoradi. The Gold Coast.

SMEDLEY: Shouldn't fancy that.

GEOFFREY: Oh, it wasn't too bad.

SMEDLEY: What are you going to do when you get back?

GEOFFREY: Well, I've got to find a job, eventually.

SMEDLEY: That shouldn't be difficult, not for a qualified chap like yourself.

GEOFFREY: I hope not.

SMEDLEY: I suppose you know a lot of people; got some pretty good contacts?

GEOFFREY: (*Hesitantly*) I've got one or two letters to various people, but –

SMEDLEY: (*Obviously becoming interested in GEOFFREY*) Do you live in London?

GEOFFREY: No.

SMEDLEY: Well, what part do you come from?

GEOFFREY: I was born in New Zealand, but my people moved to England when I was sixteen, that was in 1930.

SMEDLEY: Are your folks still alive?

GEOFFREY: No, they were both killed in a motor car accident …

SMEDLEY: Oh, I'm sorry.

GEOFFREY: It seems a long time now. (*He lights his cigarette*) I suppose it is a long time ago, it's over twenty years.

There is a knock on the door and a WAITER enters with the coffee etc on a tray.

WAITER: On the table, sir?

GEOFFREY: (*Nodding*) Please …

The WAITER puts the tray down on the table and then goes out.

GEOFFREY: (*To SMEDLEY*) Do you happen to know a hotel in London called the Granchester?

SMEDLEY: Yes, I think so. It's in Southampton Row.

GEOFFREY: What's it like?

SMEDLEY: Oh, I wouldn't know. Are you staying there?

GEOFFREY: It's been recommended to me; but I shall get a flat as soon as I can.

SMEDLEY: (*Laughing*) You mean, you'll try to get one.

GEOFFREY pours out the coffee.

GEOFFREY: Yes, I suppose it's not very easy.

SMEDLEY takes his coffee from GEOFFREY.

SMEDLEY: Haven't you any brothers or sisters you could stay with?

GEOFFREY: No.

SMEDLEY: (*Smiling; stirring his coffee*) You're a bit of a lone wolf.

GEOFFREY: Yes, I suppose I am.

SMEDLEY: You know what you want …

GEOFFREY: (*Faintly amused*) No, what do I want?

SMEDLEY: You want a nice cosy little flat and a nice cosy little girl friend.

GEOFFREY: I'll settle for the flat.

SMEDLEY: Why, don't you like women?

GEOFFREY: I'm afraid I haven't had a lot of experience.

SMEDLEY: You don't have to have experience to like 'em. It's when you've had the experience that you don't like them!

GEOFFREY laughs and picks up a slip of paper off the tray. He feels in his pocket. SMEDLEY takes the paper out of GEOFFREY's hand.

SMEDLEY: Here, I'll take that. (*He looks at the bill and picks up his wallet*) What's this – three hundred francs for two coffees? (*He looks at GEOFFREY*) Seems a bit steep, doesn't it?

GEOFFREY: Well –

SMEDLEY: (*Opening his wallet*) Perhaps you're right. (*He feels his chin and smiles at GEOFFREY*) We won't argue.

CUT TO: The Reception Desk in the Hall of the Hotel. Next morning.

People are arriving; checking out; inquiring for messages, letters, etc. A pretty looking girl, dressed as a NURSE, flits backwards and forwards. She is selling flags in aid of a local hospital. There is a table displaying the flags and a poster for the hospital.

WALTER SMEDLEY arrives; he is wearing the same suit as the night before, but he has a trilby on the back of his head and carries a briefcase. He now looks alert and business-like.

SMEDLEY: (*To the RECEPTIONIST*) Good morning!

RECEPTIONIST: Good morning, sir!

SMEDLEY: I phoned down for my bill about ten minutes ago – Smedley …

RECEPTIONIST: That's right, sir. (*Turns and picks up SMEDLEY's account from a pile of papers*) It's ready for you …

SMEDLEY: Good … (*He takes out his wallet and after examining the statement places a pile of notes on the reception desk*) Has Mr Ryder left yet – Room 82?

RECEPTIONIST: (*Picking up the notes and the account*) I don't think so, sir – he was here a few moments ago.

SMEDLEY: Ring his room, will you, please?

RECEPTIONIST: The concierge will do that, monsieur.

The RECEPTIONIST puts SMEDLEY's change and receipt on the desk. The GIRL approaches and offers SMEDLEY a flag.

GIRL: (*Smiling*) If you please, monsieur …

SMEDLEY: (*Placing a note in the collection box the GIRL is carrying*) What's this in aid of – retired champagne merchants?

The GIRL smiles and pins a flag to his lapel.

GEOFFREY arrives; he already wears a flag in his buttonhole and carries his hat and coat.

GEOFFREY: Good morning!

SMEDLEY: (*Pleased to see GEOFFREY*) Oh, hello! I was just inquiring about you.

GEOFFREY: What time does your train leave?

SMEDLEY: Nine fifteen, I think it is, from the Gare d'Lyon. (*He takes GEOFFREY by the arm*) Look, I want to have a little talk with you. Come and sit down for a minute!

GEOFFREY and SMEDLEY cross the hall towards two armchairs and a small table. As they sit in the armchairs, GEOFFREY takes out his cigarette case.

SMEDLEY: (*Refusing a cigarette*) No, I won't, thanks very much. My throat's a bit funny this morning. (*He glances at his wristwatch*) My goodness, I haven't a lot of time.

GEOFFREY: Have they brought your luggage down?

SMEDLEY: Yes, it's outside – they're getting me a taxi. (*Turning towards GEOFFREY*) Now look, Mr Ryder, I did a spot of thinking when I got to bed last night, and it dawned on Walter Smedley Esquire that he'd have been in a pretty nasty hole if it hadn't been for you.

GEOFFREY: Oh, I don't know about that …

SMEDLEY: Well, I do. If you hadn't have taken me under your wing, I should have probably taken a poke at that dressed up monkey

20

	and – well, there'd have been fireworks all round. Wouldn't have done me any good.
GEOFFREY:	(*Smiling*) It wouldn't have done him any good either.
SMEDLEY:	Yes, I know, but our Chairman's pretty strait-laced. It wouldn't have been so funny if I'd landed up in jug. Anyway, that's not what I wanted to talk to you about. I've got a flat in London, in Knightsbridge, I think I mentioned it last night …
GEOFFREY:	Yes, you did.
SMEDLEY:	Well, if you've no place to go in London, and you said you hadn't, I don't see why you shouldn't move in there. It's all ready for you, furnished and everything …
GEOFFREY:	You mean – take the flat over, while you're away?
SMEDLEY:	That's right – it'll be for about six months.
GEOFFREY:	Well, that's awfully good of you, but – (*Hesitantly*) What sort of rent have you got in mind, Mr Smedley?
SMEDLEY:	I haven't got any rent in mind. I'm not worried about the rent, old man! If I'd wanted to have let the place, I could have let it fifty times over.
GEOFFREY:	Yes, I appreciate that, but if I'm going to take it, I've got to have some idea …
SMEDLEY:	(*His hand on GEOFFREY's knee*) Look, you did me a favour last night, Ryder – now I'm doing you one. At least, I hope I am.
GEOFFREY:	Yes, of course you are. I shall be very glad to rent it off you if it's …

21

SMEDLEY: (*Amused*) Don't worry your head about the rent, we can discuss that when I'm back in London.

GEOFFREY: I – I don't know what to say …

SMEDLEY: You don't have to say anything. And for goodness' sake, don't feel you're under any obligation. If you must know, you'll be doing me a favour by keeping an eye on the place.

A UNIFORMED PORTER arrives and speaks to SMEDLEY.

PORTER: (*To SMEDLEY*) Your car is ready, monsieur.

SMEDLEY: (*To the PORTER*) All right, I'll be out in a minute.

The PORTER leaves.

SMEDLEY: (*Taking a piece of paper out of his waistcoat pocket*) Now look, I've scribbled two addresses on this piece of paper.

GEOFFREY takes the piece of paper.

SMEDLEY: One's my address in Genoa, and the other's my sister's – she lives in Putney.

GEOFFREY: (*Looking at the paper*) Mrs Katherine Weldon …

SMEDLEY: That's right. When you get to London give her a ring and she'll meet you and take you out to the flat. She's got the keys.

GEOFFREY: But won't she think it rather odd when a complete stranger …

SMEDLEY: (*Grinning*) I phoned her last night and said you'd probably be getting in touch – she knows all about it.

GEOFFREY: (*Amused*) Well – thanks.

22

SMEDLEY:	(*Rising*) Oh, there's just one thing. I – er – I didn't mention that night club place. I said we'd met at a conference.
GEOFFREY:	I understand.
SMEDLEY:	And a word of warning! Her name's Katherine but don't, for goodness' sake, call her Kate – she doesn't like it.
GEOFFREY:	(*Puzzled*) Who?
SMEDLEY:	My sister!
GEOFFREY:	(*Laughing*) I wouldn't dream of calling her Kate.
SMEDLEY:	Well, you never know. (*Shaking hands*) Drop me a line, let me know how you get on …
GEOFFREY:	Yes, of course.
SMEDLEY:	(*Picking up his briefcase*) I wish to goodness I was going back with you. (*Suddenly; almost an afterthought*) Oh, before I forget! I'm in a bit of a quandary. I can't remember whether I brought my cigarette case with me or left it in the flat. If it is in the flat, I'd be awfully grateful if you'd send me a telegram.
GEOFFREY:	Yes, of course.
SMEDLEY:	I've been really worried about it. I only hope to goodness it hasn't been pinched.
GEOFFREY:	What does it look like?
SMEDLEY:	It's a gold, square-looking case. It was the last present the wife gave me. I shall be hopping mad if I've lost it.
GEOFFREY:	When did you last have it?
SMEDLEY:	I don't know, I can't remember – that's what's so damn silly!
GEOFFREY:	If it's in the flat, do you want me to send it on to you?

SMEDLEY:	No, you'd better not, there'd be too much fuss with the customs. There's a writing desk in the lounge, lock it up in that. (*He glances at his watch again*) By Jove, I'm cutting it fine!
GEOFFREY:	For Heaven's sake, don't miss your train!
SMEDLEY:	What time are you leaving?
GEOFFREY:	I'm catching the eleven o'clock plane.
SMEDLEY:	Oh, you've bags of time! Well, pick yourself a cushy job in London, and give Katherine my love!

SMEDLEY gives GEOFFREY a friendly pat on the shoulder and rises. He crosses the hall and turns and gives GEOFFREY a final little wave. GEOFFREY waves back and then turns and sits down again in one of the armchairs. He puts the piece of paper he is holding down on the table and takes out his diary and pencil. He copies the addresses into the diary and then screws the note up into a ball and tosses it into a nearby waste-paper basket. He then rises and crosses to the reception desk.

GEOFFREY's VOICE:	I have a habit of losing odd pieces of paper, so I copied the two addresses and Mrs Weldon's telephone number into my diary. After that, I paid my bill, settled a small account with the concierge, and arranged for my luggage to be brought down. Four hours later I arrived in London.

The RECEPTIONIST nods and presents GEOFFREY with his account. GEOFFREY takes his wallet out of his pocket and sorts out the various franc notes.

CUT TO: Passengers alighting from a B.E.A. Aircraft at London Airport. The group includes GEOFFREY.

CUT TO: The Interior of the Customs Hall at London Airport.

GEOFFREY's luggage is being examined by a CUSTOMS OFFICER who is quite friendly as he searches the luggage bearing the initials "G.R." GEOFFREY appears indifferent; rather bored by the proceedings. He looks about him; glancing at his watch; he notices the hospital flag still in his lapel; he takes it out of his lapel and drops it in a metal waste-paper tub at his feet. The CUSTOMS OFFICER is now satisfied with his examination; he closes the suitcase and chalks his approval on the rest of GEOFFREY's luggage.

CUT TO: The Main Exit from London Airport.

Passengers are passing to and fro. Porters with luggage; uniformed officials, air hostesses, etc. GEOFFREY appears, followed by a PORTER with his luggage. He pauses in the doorway. KATHERINE WELDON arrives and dashes into the building. Suddenly she turns, looks down at the initials on GEOFFREY's suitcase. KATHERINE is a smart, sophisticated woman in her middle thirties. GEOFFREY turns and is surprised to see KATHERINE staring at him. KATHERINE returns to where GEOFFREY is standing.

KATHERINE: I beg your pardon, but – you don't happen to be Mr Ryder, by any chance?

GEOFFREY: (*Puzzled*) Yes – my name's Ryder.

KATHERINE: Geoffrey Ryder?

GEOFFREY: Yes.

KATHERINE: (*Smiling; obviously relieved*) Well, thank goodness I've found you, Mr Ryder! I was terrified in case I'd missed you!

GEOFFREY: I'm afraid there's some mistake, you see …

KATHERINE: (*Shaking her head; laughing*) No, you don't understand. (*As if this explains everything*)

I'm leaving for Scotland tomorrow morning …

GEOFFREY: (*Politely*) Scotland?

KATHERINE: Yes.

GEOFFREY: (*A moment*) Oh.

GEOFFREY and KATHERINE smile at each other for a moment; then KATHERINE suddenly realises that GEOFFREY hasn't the slightest idea who she is.

KATHERINE: Oh, I beg your pardon! Obviously, you haven't the faintest idea who I am!

GEOFFREY: I'm afraid I haven't.

KATHERINE: I'm Katherine Weldon. My brother telephoned from Paris and …

GEOFFREY: (*Surprised; taking off his hat*) Oh, hello, Mrs Weldon! I'm delighted to meet you … (*He shakes hands with Katherine*)

KATHERINE: I'm delighted to meet you too! I felt sure I'd left it too late.

GEOFFREY: (*Puzzled*) But I didn't expect you to meet the plane. Your brother said that …

KATHERINE: Yes, I know. Walter said you'd telephone me about the flat, but I suddenly realised afterwards that I was going away tomorrow morning and that if you didn't phone today, you'd never be able to get hold of me.

GEOFFREY: Well, it was awfully kind of you to dash down here like this …

KATHERINE: (*Laughing*) I'm afraid I'd no alternative …

PORTER: (*To GEOFFREY*) Have you a car, sir?

KATHERINE: (*To the PORTER*) Yes, it's in the car park. A Rover – TPE 246. (*To GEOFFREY*) I imagine you'd like to go straight to the flat?

GEOFFREY: But isn't this frightfully inconvenient for you?

KATHERINE: It isn't a bit inconvenient – but it would have been if you'd been arriving tomorrow.

GEOFFREY: (*Smiling*) Does your brother often let you in for this sort of thing?

KATHERINE: No, this is most unlike Walter. (*Looking at GEOFFREY*) What happened in Paris, Mr Ryder?

GEOFFREY: What do you mean?

KATHERINE: Well – Walter said you'd met at a conference, but it didn't sound a very likely story.

GEOFFREY: That's what happened.

LATHERINE: (*With the suggestion of a smile*) Truly?

GEOFFREY: (*Not very convincingly*) Truly.

KATHERINE: (*Not convinced*) Well, I'll take your word for it.

CUT TO: The Living Room of the Flat.

This is a large mews flat in Knightsbridge. There is a door leading to a bedroom, and a second door leading to a bathroom and toilet. The flat is hardly any type of establishment one would associate with WALTER SMEDLEY. The furnishings are excellent, almost to the point of being luxurious. There is a beautiful writing bureau, several antique tables, a wing chair, drinks cabinet, books, tapestries, etc. The telephone is on a small table with a large silver cigarette box and a table lamp.

The door opens and KATHERINE enters closely followed by GEOFFREY.

KATHERINE: Well, I think that's the lot. You've seen just about everything … oh, before I forget! The dishwasher doesn't work, it's been disconnected.

GEOFFREY: (*Smiling*) I'll remember that.

27

KATHERINE: Oh, and I meant to ask you – did Walter say anything about a Mrs Bates?

GEOFFREY: No.

KATHERINE: Well, she's the daily help – except that she isn't very helpful. She may not even turn up.

GEOFFREY: Well, if she does, she can carry on, if not I'll get someone else …

KATHERINE: (*Laughing*) I gather you've a magic wand, Mr Ryder.

GEOFFREY smiles and looks round the room; he is obviously highly delighted with the flat.

KATHERINE: Do you like it?

GEOFFREY: (*Turning towards KATHERINE*) Like it? But it's wonderful! I never expected anything like this.

KATHERINE: (*Faintly amused*) What did you expect?

GEOFFREY: I – I don't really know. The usual bed-sitting-room, I suppose. This is absolute luxury.

KATHERINE: Didn't Walter tell you it was a very nice flat?

GEOFFREY: Yes, he did, but …

KATHERINE: But you didn't think he'd got such good taste?

GEOFFREY: (*Without thinking*) Yes – No – I mean …

KATHERINE: (*Laughing*) There's no need to be embarrassed, Mr Ryder. You're not the first person to underrate my brother. (*She nods towards a picture on the far wall*) You see that picture?

GEOFFREY crosses and looks at the picture.

KATHERINE: It's a Van Hoffman …

GEOFFREY: (*Staring at the picture*) A … Van Hoffman?

KATHERINE: (*Nodding*) Do you know how much my brother gave for it?

GEOFFREY: No …

KATHERINE: Fourteen pounds ten.

GEOFFREY: Fourteen pounds ten?

KATHERINE: Yes.

GEOFFREY: Well – er – what's it worth?

KATHERINE: About six hundred pounds.

GEOFFREY: Good heavens! (*He peers at the picture*) I say, is it really worth six hundred pounds?

KATHERINE: He was offered five hundred for it just before he left.

GEOFFREY: (*Shaking his hand*) Things like that never happen to me!

KATHERINE: (*Laughing*) Me neither!

There is a pause. GEOFFREY is still looking at the picture.

KATHERINE: What are you thinking?

GEOFFREY: I was just wondering whether I'd have given fourteen pounds ten for it.

KATHERINE laughs; she holds out her hand.

KATHERINE: Well, here's the keys, Mr Ryder. I hope you'll be very happy here.

GEOFFREY takes the keys from KATHERINE.

GEOFFREY: I'm sure I shall …

KATHERINE: I shall be away for ten days; after that, if there's anything you want just give me a ring. You've got my number.

GEOFFREY: Yes. (*He takes out his diary and glances at it*) Putney 8044 …

KATHERINE: That's it …

GEOFFREY: (*Replacing his diary*) It's really most awfully kind of you to go to all this trouble, Mrs Weldon. I'm very grateful.

KATHERINE: (*Suddenly facing GEOFFREY; smiling*) Are you really grateful?

GEOFFREY: (*A shade surprised*) Yes.

KATHERINE: Then would you do something for me?

GEOFFREY: Why – yes, of course. What is it?

KATHERINE: (*Faintly amused*) Tell me how you met Walter.

GEOFFREY: But he told you.

KATHERINE: Was it at a conference?

GEOFFREY: Why – yes …

KATHERINE: In Paris?

GEOFFREY: Right – right in the middle of Paris.

KATHERINE: But I thought Walter was going straight to Genoa? He never said anything about a conference while he was in London.

GEOFFREY: I – I think it all blew up rather suddenly.

KATHERINE: What sort of conference was it, Mr Ryder?

GEOFFREY: Why – an engineering conference.

KATHERINE: Are you an engineer?

GEOFFREY: No, I'm a metallurgical chemist.

KATHERINE: Oh, I see. (*With a little laugh*) At least, I think I see.

GEOFFREY: (*Changing the subject*) Mrs Weldon, when you get back from Scotland, I wonder if you and your husband would have dinner with me one evening?

KATHERINE: That's awfully kind of you, but – I'm afraid my husband and I don't see a great deal of each other …

GEOFFREY: Oh …

KATHERINE: We're very good friends, but we're not …

GEOFFREY: I understand. Well, perhaps you'd care to have dinner with me – without your husband?

KATHERINE: I should love to.

GEOFFREY: I'll give you a ring, (*He hesitates*) – unless, of course …

KATHERINE: Yes?

GEOFFREY: I was going to say, unless you'd like to make it this evening?

KATHERINE: (*Laughing*) That's rather short notice!

GEOFFREY: Well, why not?

KATHERINE: (*A moment*) I did intend visiting a friend of mine …

GEOFFREY: (*Smiling*) You can phone him.

KATHERINE: It's a 'she'.

GEOFFREY: All right – visit your friend and then have dinner with me.

KATHERINE: I'm afraid it might be very late.

GEOFFREY: That doesn't matter.

KATHERINE: Well …

GEOFFREY: (*With the suggestion of a smile*) If you do, I'll tell you all about the conference.

KATHERINE: (*Laughing; intrigued*) All right, Mr Ryder! Let's say nine o'clock.

GEOFFREY: Nine o'clock. The Savoy Grill?

KATHERINE: No, that's much too grand. Do you know Chez Rousseau?

GEOFFREY: (*Shaking his head*) No …

KATHERINE: It's a tiny restaurant, but it's very nice. It's in Charlotte Street.

GEOFFREY: I'll find it. (*He smiles at KATHERINE*) Nine o'clock.

KATHERINE smiles back at GEOFFREY.

CUT TO: GEOFFREY's open suitcase containing pyjamas, underwear, ties, socks, etc.

GEOFFREY enters the living room from the bathroom and then crosses to the bedroom and the open suitcase. He has taken off his jacket and loosened his tie; he looks very pleased with himself. He starts to take things out of the suitcase, placing them in a nearby chest of drawers. He finds a packet

31

of cigarettes in the suitcase, and this immediately reminds him of WALTER SMEDLEY's request concerning the lost cigarette case.

GEOFFREY's VOICE: I was in pretty high spirits that afternoon. The flat was very much nicer than I'd expected and Mrs Weldon – well, she was very much nicer, too. I thanked my lucky stars I'd had the good sense to call in Paris on the way home. Then suddenly, while I was unpacking, I remembered the lost cigarette case and the promise I had made to Walter Smedley.

GEOFFREY turns from the bed and commences to search the bedroom. It doesn't reveal the cigarette case, so GEOFFREY goes into the living room where he goes across to the writing bureau. He opens it (the key is in the lock) and searches, without success. He closes the bureau and turns towards a small drawer in one of the occasional tables. The case is not in the drawer. GEOFFREY is closing the drawer when the telephone rings. GEOFFREY goes across to the table and picks up the receiver. During the conversation we hear DAVID WELDON's voice, but we do not see him. The voice is well educated, with the suggestion of a drawl.

DAVID's VOICE: Hello? … Is that Knightsbridge 1934?

GEOFFREY: (*Looking at the telephone dial*) Er – yes.

DAVID: Could I speak to Mrs Weldon please?

GEOFFREY: I'm sorry, but Mrs Weldon isn't here at the moment.

DAVID: Oh. Oh, I beg your pardon. I understood she was calling on you this afternoon …

GEOFFREY: Yes – she was here a few moments ago, you've only just missed her.

DAVID: Oh. Oh dear, how very tiresome! (*Quite pleasantly*) Well, thank you so much. I'm very sorry to have troubled you.

GEOFFREY: Is there any message?

DAVID: Well – (*Fairly curious*) Will you be seeing her again then?

GEOFFREY: Yes, she's dining with me this evening.

DAVID: Oh – Well, in that case would you ask her to give me a ring?

GEOFFREY: Yes, certainly.

DAVID: Jolly good …

GEOFFREY: Who shall I say called?

DAVID: (*A moment*) Her husband.

David replaces the receiver.

GEOFFREY looks at the telephone; surprised. Then he smiles, gives a little shrug and replaces the receiver. He opens the large silver box on the table and puts his hand inside for a cigarette, his thoughts still on the phone call. Suddenly, his expression changes and he looks down at the box. Inside the box is Walter Smedley's cigarette case. Geoffrey takes the case out of the box and examines it, turning it over in his hand. He does not open it. The case is exactly as WALTER described it.

He takes the cigarette case to the writing bureau; he locks it in the bureau and puts the key in his pocket. Having done this, he returns to the telephone and after taking out his pocket diary, lifts the telephone receiver and dials.

OPERATOR: (*On the other end of the line*) Overseas Telegrams …

GEOFFREY: I want to send a telegram to Genoa, Italy …

OPERATOR: Yes … Can I have your number, please?

GEOFFREY: (*Looking at the telephone dial*) Knightsbridge 1934.

OPERATOR: Thank you.

33

We hear the tap-tap of a typewriter.

GEOFFREY: (*Looking at his diary*) It's to Walter Smedley ... Hotel Excelsior Vittoria ... Genoa ...

OPERATOR: (*After a pause*) Yes ...

GEOFFREY: (*Smiling; speaking slowly*) Have met your charming sister and found your cigarette case. Delighted with the flat ... Regards ... Geoffrey Ryder ...

CUT TO: Chez Rousseau Restaurant.

A WAITER is preparing coffee on a side table. At a small corner table, KATHERINE and GEOFFREY sit; they have finished their dinner and are having their coffee. KATHERINE is obviously amused by what GEOFFREY has said; they are now quite friendly.

KATHERINE: I never did believe that nonsense about a conference! I knew perfectly well Walter wasn't telling the truth ... But tell me, what happened about the champagne – did he pay?

GEOFFREY: I'm afraid he did. The waiter said "Eleven thousand francs, monsieur" and I simply took it out of the wallet.

KATHERINE: Good for you! It just serves Walter right. You know, he's always doing that sort of thing. He gets terribly aggressive and then acts rather like an overgrown schoolboy.

GEOFFREY: To be fair to him, I don't think this was entirely his fault; they really were taking him for a ride. (*Suddenly*) Have some more coffee, Mrs Weldon?

KATHERINE: No, thank you, Mr Ryder.

GEOFFREY: You're quite sure, Mrs Weldon?

KATHERINE: I'm quite sure, Mr Ryder.

GEOFFREY: (*Laughing*) The name's Geoffrey ...

KATHERINE: Katherine …

GEOFFREY: I know; Katherine, but not Kate.

KATHERINE: (*Surprised*) Who told you that – Walter?

GEOFFREY: Yes. Why don't you like Kate? I think it's such an attractive name.

KATHERINE: It always make me think of antimacassars and barley sugar.

GEOFFREY: Why barley sugar, for goodness sake?

KATHERINE: (*Shaking her head; amused*) I don't know, but it does! It always has done, ever since I was a little girl. Besides David calls me Kate …

GEOFFREY: David?

KATHERINE: My husband …

GEOFFREY: (*Suddenly*) Oh, good lord, I forgot to tell you! He telephoned, just after you left.

KATHERINE: Yes, I know, I've spoken to him.

GEOFFREY: He sounded awfully nice on the telephone.

KATHERINE: He is awfully nice – on the telephone. (*Shaking her head*) No, I suppose that's a little unfair. He's a very nice person altogether, but – well, it just didn't work out.

GEOFFREY: What does he do? Is he in business?

KATHERINE: Good heavens, no! He doesn't do anything. That's the trouble; he's terribly well off and he's bone idle.

GEOFFREY: But he must do something.

KATHERINE: (*A shrug*) He goes to his tailors, his club, the theatre; reads quite a lot. He's perfectly happy; quite contented. Everything's (*Imitating DAVID*) – jolly good.

GEOFFREY: But has he always been like that?

KATHERINE: (*Thoughtfuly*) Yes, I think he has. I believe originally he toyed with the idea of going into the Diplomatic Service but …

GEOFFREY: He wasn't diplomatic …
KATHERINE: Oh, he was diplomatic all right, but he just wouldn't work.
GEOFFREY: Anyway, obviously, you're quite good friends.
KATHERINE: Oh, yes. Ex-wife lunches with ex-husband. It's all perfectly civilised. I don't think we've ever had a decent, respectable row.
GEOFFREY: (*Smiling*) Does he live in Town?
KATHERINE: Yes, he's got a house in Mount Street.
GEOFFREY: And you're out at Putney.
KATHERINE: Yes – on the heath. The Seventy-Four passes the door.
GEOFFREY: How very stupid of the Seventy-Four.
KATHERINE: (*Glancing at her watch; amused*) Mr Ryder, I think that's my exit line!
GEOFFREY: No, no, don't go, please! Have some more coffee?
KATHERINE: (*Laughing; hesitating*) Well –
GEOFFREY: (*Beckoning*) Waiter …
KATHERINE: Tell me; what are you going to do while you're in London? Visit Madame Tussaud's, the Tower of London?
GEOFFREY: Good heavens, no! I'm not on a sight-seeing tour. I've got to find myself a job!
KATHERINE: Will that be difficult?
GEOFFREY: It's hard to say. I don't really think so, on the other hand I don't know many people and it's a long time since I was over here.
KATHERINE: Well, I expect you've made some contacts?
GEOFFREY: Yes, of course. I'm seeing several people this week as a matter of fact.
KATHERINE: (*Facing him*) Supposing you could do exactly what you wanted?

GEOFFREY: Well?

KATHERINE: Well – what would you do?

GEOFFREY: Exactly what I wanted?

KATHERINE: Yes.

GEOFFREY: I'd work at Stanfield.

KATHERINE: What's that?

GEOFFREY: It's a Government Research Laboratory.

KATHERINE: In London?

GEOFFREY: No, it's just outside Guildford. It's a small experimental place but they're doing a certain amount of work on powder metallurgy, and that's what I'm chiefly interested in.

KATHERINE: Powder metallurgy. What's that?

GEOFFREY: Well, it's ………………………………………

KATHERINE: Oh, you mean ……………………..

GEOFFREY: M'm – yes …………………………………

KATHERINE: A sort of ……………………………….

(FD note: The above lines need to be completed – technical research needs to be done.)

GEOFFREY: (*Laughing*) I can see you've got the whole thing at your fingertips.

KATHERINE: Don't you know anyone at Stanfield?

GEOFFREY: I wrote to Dr Elroyd about two months ago – he's the head of the Experimental Section.

KATHERINE: What happened?

GEOFFREY: I didn't even get a reply.

KATHERINE: Well, isn't there anyone else there?

GEOFFREY: There's Sir Carl Melford, he's Chairman of the Advisory Committee.

KATHERINE: Have you written to him?

GEOFFREY: Yes. I had a delightful letter from his secretary. A Miss Primrose. She said, nothing doing. Which is exactly what you'd expect of course from a young lady called Primrose.

KATHERINE laughs. GEOFFREY looks round and beckons the WAITER again.

KATHERINE: Geoffrey, do you mind if I don't have any more coffee?

GEOFFREY: No, of course not.

KATHERINE: I'd really like to be making a move …

GEOFFREY: Really?

KATHERINE: My train goes awfully early tomorrow, and I've still got some packing to do.

GEOFFREY: Yes, all right.

The WAITER comes to the table.

WAITER: Yes, sir?

GEOFFREY: (*Looking at KATHERINE*) My bill, please.

WAITER: L'addition?

GEOFFREY: (*Turning toward the WAITER*) I beg your pardon?

WAITER: L'addition, monsieur.

GEOFFREY: Oh, yes – yes, that's right. L'addition.

GEOFFREY looks at KATHERINE and laughs.

CUT TO: The Flat. The Living Room.

GEOFFREY enters; he switches on the light. He is wearing an overcoat and carries a soft hat. He takes off his coat and puts it, together with his hat, on the wing chair. He then loosens his tie and crosses towards the bedroom. He hesitates by the table and looks down at the table lamp and the silver cigarette box. He has noticed that the box has been moved slightly. He turns and looks towards the writing bureau and the drinks cabinet; he then looks round the room, hesitates again, gives a faint shrug and continues towards the bedroom.

CUT TO: The Flat.   The Bedroom.

STELLA, a dark, efficient looking girl in the late twenties, is searching the chest of drawers. She suddenly hears GEOFFREY and, taking her handbag from the chest of drawers, she turns and flattens herself against the wall. As she does so the door opens, and GEOFFREY comes into the room. He switches on the light and stops dead at the sight of the dishevelled chest of drawers. He goes across to it and looks down at the half open, partly ransacked drawer. STELLA is standing tense and rigid watching GEOFFREY. After a moment, she moves from behind the door and with her eyes still on GEOFFREY she crosses towards the living room. Suddenly, GEOFFREY turns and as he does so, STELLA runs through the bedroom door and across the living room. GEOFFREY springs forward in pursuit of her.

CUT TO: The Flat.   The Living Room.

STELLA races across the living room towards the hall. GEOFFREY catches up with her before she reaches the hall, making a grab for her dress. STELLA turns and strikes out, taking GEOFFREY by surprise. He falls backwards, clutching STELLA's arm and handbag in an attempt to steady himself. The situation is not entirely new to the girl; she is tense and desperately determined to escape, but there is no sign of panic.

GEOFFREY regains his balance and makes another attempt to hold STELLA, but she is now in command of the situation and forces him backwards against the table. As Geoffrey tries to regain his balance again the girl picks up the table lamp and clubs him across the head. He falls backwards, still clutching her handbag, and finally drops to the floor. By the time GEOFFREY has hit the floor the girl has already departed.

GEOFFREY is dazed and confused, but not badly hurt. After a while he rises and stands by the table holding his head. He stares down at the table, then slowly picks up the lamp and places it next to the telephone. He then realises that he is holding the girl's handbag. He rests the handbag on the table, opens it, and tips out the contents. The bag contains a powder compact, a handkerchief, a lipstick holder, a bunch of keys, a wallet and a small Leica camera; there is also a tiny flashbulb.

GEOFFREY picks up the camera and carefully examines it; holding it up to his eyes to examine the viewfinder. He then puts the camera down on the table and picks up the bulb. He looks at the bulb and at the table lamp and picks up the camera again; after a moment, he turns the exposure winder, releases the back of the camera, and extracts the exposed film. He flicks the tab down on the film and, after a momentary hesitation, puts it in his pocket. He closes the camera and together with the bulb and other articles, replaces it in the handbag; he then picks up the telephone receiver and starts to dial a number.

CUT TO: The Flat. The Bedroom.

DETECTIVE SERGEANT GORRINGE is testing the chest of drawers for fingerprints. He has the usual white powder and fingerprint paraphernalia. DETECTIVE INSPECTOR MANN is standing at the foot of the bed holding the handbag and watching SERGEANT GORRINGE who straightens himself and points to a patch of white powder on the chest of drawers.

GORRINGE: That's the only one, I'm afraid, sir. It's not very good.

MANN: The times I've heard you say that, Sergeant. All right – leave it and try the rest of the room.

GORRINGE: What about the handbag, sir?

MANN: (*Shaking his head*) I'm taking it down to the Station.

GORRINGE: There may be something on the camera.

MANN: You can test it later.

GORRINGE: (*Nodding*) Yes, sir.

INSPECTOR MANN leaves the bedroom.

CUT TO: The Flat. The Living Room.

INSPECTOR MANN enters from the bedroom. GEOFFREY is standing near the drinks cabinet with a whisky and soda in his hand.

GEOFFREY: (*Indicating his drink*) Would you like one, Inspector?

MANN: No, sir – not at the moment, thank you. (*He looks at GEOFFREY; he hesitates*) Mr Ryder, how old would you say this girl was?

GEOFFREY: Oh, about twenty-seven or eight.

MANN: (*Looking down at the handbag he is holding*) Would you recognise her again?

GEOFFREY: (*Hesitantly*) Yes – I think so.

MANN: But you're not sure?

GEOFFREY: Well, it all happened so quickly. One minute she was in the bedroom, the next minute we were in here having a free for all.

MANN: (*Smiling*) Yes. I suppose it's difficult to get a good look at the girl under those circumstances. (*He looks at the bag again*) Did you examine the handbag, Mr Ryder?

GEOFFREY: Yes.

MANN: (*Casually*) She was carrying a camera.

GEOFFREY: Yes, I know.

MANN: Have you any idea why?

GEOFFREY: I haven't the faintest idea why. (*Faintly exasperated*) I've told you what happened,

41

	Inspector. She was searching the flat, I disturbed her, and she made a dash for it.
MANN:	(*Thoughtfully*) Yes … (*Suddenly*) This friend of yours, Mr – er – Headley …
GEOFFREY:	Smedley. Walter Smedley.
MANN:	Ah, yes, Mr Smedley! Is he the landlord, sir, or just the tenant?
GEOFFREY:	I – I imagine he's the tenant.
MANN:	(*Nodding*) So you're on a sub-let?
GEOFFREY:	I suppose you could call it that. (*Faintly irritated*) But I told you what happened, Inspector. I did Smedley a favour and he returned it by letting me have the flat.
MANN:	(*Non-committally*) Yes, you told me, sir.
GEOFFREY:	Of course, this burglary business is very awkward because I don't really know whether she's taken anything or not.
MANN:	(*Looking round the flat*) Do you think she has, sir?
GEOFFREY:	Frankly, I don't know. (*He puts his glass down*) There's plenty of things she could have taken, but obviously didn't.
MANN:	Such as …?

GEOFFREY crosses to the writing bureau.

GEOFFREY:	Well, there was a gold cigarette case in the bureau. (*He opens the desk*) It's still here.

The INSPECTOR joins GEOFFREY and looks down into the writing bureau.

MANN:	Did she open the desk?
GEOFFREY:	Yes.
MANN:	How do you know?
GEOFFREY:	It was unlocked, but I distinctly remember locking it before I went out. (*He takes the key from his waistcoat*) Here's the key …

42

MANN looks at GEOFFREY for a moment, then opens the handbag and takes out the bunch of keys. He tries the keys in the bureau; there is one that definitely fits. He looks up at GEOFFREY and nods.

MANN: (*Indicating the cigarette case*) I take it the case is Mr Smedley's?

GEOFFREY: Of course.

MANN: I wonder why he left it behind?

GEOFFREY: He didn't, he mislaid it – as a matter of fact he thought he'd lost it.

The INSPECTOR nods and closes the bureau; replacing the keys in the handbag.

MANN: I gather you haven't missed anything, sir.

GEOFFREY: No, I've been through all my stuff, there's nothing missing.

MANN: Good. (*Suddenly; pleasantly dismissing the matter*) Well, thank you, Mr Ryder. You've been most helpful. Oh, I think you said you'd got Mr Smedley's address.

GEOFFREY: Yes.

MANN takes an envelope and a pencil from his inside pocket.

MANN: Can I have it, please, sir?

GEOFFREY: Yes, certainly. He's staying at the Excelsior Vittoria Hotel, Genoa …

MANN: (*Starting to write it down*) The Excelsior Vitto … (*He offers GEOFFREY the envelope and pencil*) Perhaps you'd be good enough to write it down for me, sir.

GEOFFREY smiles and takes the envelope and pencil.

CUT TO: Against a dark bathroom background – a developing tank, a beaker of water, photographic materials etc.

GEOFFREY's VOICE: I don't know why I didn't tell the Inspector about the film; my behaviour was stupid and irresponsible, and I've regretted it ever since. But I was curious. I felt convinced that the girl had broken into the flat for a particular reason and I wondered if, by any chance, I should discover that reason if I developed the film. The next morning, I bought the necessary materials and blacked-out the bathroom.

GEOFFREY's hands appear holding the film. He releases the film into the tank; pours powder into the beaker, mixes the powder and water, and commences the developing process.

CUT TO: The Flat. The Living Room.
GEOFFREY comes out of the bathroom with his sleeves rolled up and holding the two negatives. He puts one on the writing bureau and holds the other one up to the light.

GEOFFREY's VOICE: It took me about five minutes to develop the film and about five seconds to discover that only two photographs had been taken. Whether they had been taken in the flat or not was impossible to say.

We see the first negative. It is as described by GEOFFREY.

GEOFFREY's VOICE: One was a photograph of a document; a Sleeper reservation from Calais to Rome, made out to Walter Smedley for the night of October 8th, which was the following Friday.

44

GEOFFREY picks up the second negative and examines it, holding it up to the light.

GEOFFREY's VOICE: The other was a map. It looked as if it had been torn from a Guide Book and a place called Torello was underlined. Across the top of the page someone had scribbled the words … "Twenty Minutes From Rome".

GEOFFREY looks thoughtful, a shade worried. He crosses to the telephone on the table and picks up the receiver and dials. We hear the number ringing out at the other end, then the receiver being lifted.

GORRINGE: (*On the other end of the phone*) Knightsbridge Police Station. Sergeant Gorringe speaking.

GEOFFREY: I want to speak to Inspector Mann, please.

GORRINGE: I'm sorry, sir, but he's out at the moment. Can I take a message?

GEOFFREY: Well – tell him Mr Ryder called.

GORRINGE: Yes, sir. Can I get him to ring you back? He shouldn't be very long, sir.

GEOFFREY: No, I've an appointment at eleven o'clock. I'll ring later.

GORRINGE: Very good, sir. (*He replaces the receiver*)

GEOFFREY replaces the receiver and turns towards the bedroom.

CUT TO: The Flat. The Bedroom.

GEOFFREY enters still holding the negatives. He crosses and takes a suitcase from under the bed; he opens the case and puts the two negatives inside. He closes the case, takes a bunch of keys from his pocket, locks the case and replaces it under the bed. He then crosses to the chest of drawers and takes out a clean shirt; he pulls his shirt out of his trousers and starts to unbutton it.

CUT TO: A block of offices in the Strand.

GEOFFREY's VOICE: I had an appointment with the Works Director of the G.L. Combine, but my mind wasn't on the interview, and I didn't give a very good account of myself. I left the office at about a quarter past twelve.

GEOFFREY emerges and walks down the Strand towards Trafalgar Square. He looks very tired; faintly dejected.

GEOFFREY's VOICE: I intended to have lunch in Soho but when I reached Cambridge Circus, I started to feel cold and miserable, and I decided to return to the flat.

GEOFFREY crosses Cambridge Circus towards Dean Street; he suddenly hesitates and hails a passing taxi. The taxi draws up to the kerb near GEOFFREY.

CUT TO: The Flat. The Living Room.

GEOFFREY's VOICE: It was one o'clock when I reached the flat and by this time I was feeling distinctly off colour. I began to wonder whether I was in for another bout of malaria.

GEOFFREY enters; he takes off his hat and coat and then crosses to the drinks cabinet and mixes himself a whisky and soda. He is obviously not feeling very well.

CUT TO: The Flat. The Bedroom.

GEOFFREY enters and takes the suitcase out from under the bed. He puts his drink down on the side table near the bed, and then takes out his bunch of keys. He is about to unlock the suitcase when the telephone rings. He hesitates, puts the keys back in his pocket and returns to the living room.

CUT TO: The Flat. The Living Room.
GEOFFREY enters and crosses to the telephone and lifts the receiver.

GEOFFREY: (*On the phone*) Hello?
MANN: (*On the other end*) Is that Mr Ryder?
GEOFFREY: Yes.
MANN: This is Inspector Mann. I believe you phoned me this morning, sir.
GEOFFREY: Yes, I did, Inspector. I'd like to see you.
MANN: Yes, of course. Is it important?
GEOFFREY: (*Slowly*) Yes, I rather think it is.
MANN: All right. I'll come round straight away.
GEOFFREY: Thank you.
MANN: (*A sudden thought*) You – you haven't had another visitor, sir?
GEOFFREY: No, no, nothing like that. (*Hesitantly*) I've got something I want to show you.
MANN: (*Interested*) Oh?
GEOFFREY: I'm afraid I ought to have shown it to you last night, Inspector.
MANN: (*Politely*) Really, sir? (*A moment*) I'll be round right away. (*He replaces the receiver*)

GEOFFREY looks at the receiver, then slowly replaces it.

CUT TO: The Flat. The Bedroom.
GEOFFREY enters and takes out his keys and opens the suitcase. He stares at it in bewilderment. The case is empty – the negatives have disappeared.

CUT TO: The Flat. The Living Room.

GEOFFREY enters from the bedroom, carrying his drink. He looks desperately worried.

GEOFFREY's VOICE: I was in a very awkward situation. Apart from being responsible for the loss of the negatives, I'd already told the Inspector that I'd discovered something of importance.

GEOFFREY crosses to the cabinet and mixes himself another drink; he sits on the arm of a chair for a moment then paces restlessly across the room; he glances at his wristlet watch; takes out his cigarette case and lights a cigarette. After a restless moment, he stubs out the cigarette in an ashtray and sits in one of the armchairs. He sinks down in the chair, obviously not feeling well. Suddenly, his expression changes, he has noticed something on the carpet near the table. He very slowly rises and crosses the room to the stretch of carpet at the foot of the table.

GEOFFREY's VOICE: It was while I was trying to decide whether I should tell the Inspector the truth or not that I noticed the flag.

There is a small white pin-flag on the carpet. GEOFFREY picks it up and looks at it thoughtfully and is definitely puzzled.

GEOFFREY's VOICE: I thought at first it was the one I'd bought in Paris. It looked exactly the same and it had the name of the hospital on it. Then suddenly I remembered that I'd thrown my flag away at London Airport. This couldn't possibly be the same one …

CUT TO: The Flat. The Front Door.

DETECTIVE INSPECTOR MANN has arrived and is ringing the bell. He wears a light overcoat – not a mackintosh – and carries a soft hat. The door is opened by GEOFFREY.

MANN: Good afternoon, Mr Ryder.

GEOFFREY: Oh, hello, Inspector. Come inside …

CUT TO: The Flat. The Living Room.

The INSPECTOR enters, followed by GEOFFREY.

MANN: It's not a very nice day, sir.

GEOFFREY: No, I'm afraid it isn't.

GEOFFREY hesitates; he looks worried, a shade uncertain of himself. He takes out his cigarette case.

GEOFFREY: Will you have a cigarette?

MANN: No, thank you.

GEOFFREY helps himself to a cigarette and MANN takes out his lighter.

MANN: (*Offering GEOFFREY a light*) Forgive my saying so, Mr Ryder, but you don't look very well …

GEOFFREY: (*His hand shaking as he accepts the light*) No, I'm not feeling too good.

MANN: (*Replacing his lighter*) I expect the climate's getting you down, it must be quite a change from South Africa.

GEOFFREY: West Africa …

MANN: Yes, of course! Takoradi, the Gold Coast.

GEOFFREY: That's right. I've had two bouts of malaria in the last eighteen months. I hope to goodness I'm not going to get another.

MANN: I hope not, sir. (*A moment*) You said there was something you wanted to show me – something you ought to have shown me last night.

49

GEOFFREY: (*Hesitantly*) Yes – yes, that's right, Inspector.
               (*He crosses to the table and picks up the flag*)
               After you left here last night, I found this, it
               was on the carpet … (*He points*) near the
               table …

*The INSPECTOR takes the flag from GEOFFREY and
examines it.*

MANN: (*Reading the name on the flag*) Hospital …
               Pasteur. (*He looks up*) Is that in Paris?
GEOFFREY: Yes.
MANN: Go on, Mr Ryder.
GEOFFREY: They were selling those flags in the hotel the
               morning I left Paris. I bought one, so did Mr
               Smedley.
MANN: (*Looking at the flag again*) I see. (*He looks up
               at GEOFFREY; apparently not seeing the
               point*) Well?
GEOFFREY: Well, I don't quite see how that flag got into
               this flat, do you, Inspector?
MANN: (*Smiling*) It's probably the one you bought,
               sir.
GEOFFREY: Oh, no, it isn't.
MANN: (*Politely*) How do you know it isn't?
GEOFFREY: Because I threw mine away.
MANN: When?
GEOFFREY: Yesterday afternoon. I remember doing it. I
               was at London Airport.
MANN: (*Turning the flag round between his fingers*)
               Are you sure?
GEOFFREY: Yes, I'm absolutely sure.

There is a slight pause.

MANN: (*Quite friendly, holding up the flag*) I think
               this must be the one you bought, sir.

GEOFFREY: (*Irritated; obviously not feeling at all well*) But it isn't! I've told you, I distinctly remember throwing mine away …

MANN: (*Indicating the pin in the flag*) The pin's quite sharp, you know – it could have caught on your overcoat, in which case …

GEOFFREY: It didn't catch on anything! I distinctly remember dropping the flag in a metal tub. You know the sort of thing, for cigarette ends …

MANN: Well, if this isn't your flag how did it get here?

GEOFFREY: Exactly!

MANN: Are you suggesting that the girl dropped it?

GEOFFREY: (*Putting his hand on his forehead, facing MANN*) I'm not suggesting anything. I'm simply telling you that I found it in the flat. You can draw your own conclusion, Inspector.

MANN: (*After a moment*) You say Mr Smedley bought one?

GEOFFREY: (*Thoughtfully*) He had one in his lapel when I said goodbye to him.

MANN looks at GEOFFREY, then nods, takes out his wallet and puts the flag inside.

MANN: All right, sir – thank you very much. (*Looking at GEOFFREY; a shade disarming*) There's nothing else?

GEOFFREY: (*Slightly taken aback*) What do you mean?

MANN: (*Pleasantly*) There's nothing else you want to tell me, sir?

GEOFFREY: No, nothing …

The INSPECTOR turns and crosses towards the door. GEOFFREY follows.

MANN: (*Turning*) We'd like you to drop in the station one afternoon, – any time it's convenient.

GEOFFREY: (*Puzzled*) Yes, certainly.

MANN: (*Smiling*) I imagine you've no objection to having your fingerprints taken?

GEOFFREY: No, I've no objection, but –

MANN: (*Smiling at GEOFFREY*) You don't have to have them taken if you don't want to, sir.

GEOFFREY: That's all right, Inspector.

MANN: (*Still smiling*) There's no hurry.

CUT TO: The Front Door of the Flat.

GEOFFREY is standing inside; the INSPECTOR is in the open doorway.

GEOFFREY: Why do you want my fingerprints, Inspector?

MANN: We found one or two prints on the camera. (*Politely*) You did touch the camera, sir?

GEOFFREY: … Yes.

MANN: (*Nodding*) We'd like to identify them.

GEOFFREY: Well, obviously if they're not my fingerprints they belong to the girl. Surely you can tell the difference?

MANN: (*Pleasantly*) We can, sir – but we'd like to make certain. (*He looks at Geoffrey; appearing quite concerned*) You look to me as if you've got a temperature. If I were you, I'd get hold of a doctor, sir.

GEOFFREY: (*Nodding*) I'll be all right. I'll take some aspirin and go to bed for an hour or two.

MANN: I think I would, sir.

GEOFFREY: Thank you for calling, Inspector.

MANN: (*Nodding; quite friendly*) Goodbye, Mr Ryder.

The INSPECTOR leaves and GEOFFREY closes the front door.

CUT TO: The Flat. The Bedroom.

GEOFFREY's VOICE: I was feeling pretty awful, but I didn't want to call a doctor. I know that if I did, he'd put me to bed for a couple of days and that was the last thing I wanted. I had a very important appointment the following afternoon.

GEOFFREY enters and crosses to the open suitcase; he stares down at the case then closes it and replaces it under the bed. As he straightens himself, he sways slightly and takes hold of the bed for support. He waits a moment then walks very unsteadily towards his dressing gown which is on the back of a chair. He takes off his jacket and puts on the dressing gown, then he returns to the bed. He sits on the bed and puts his head in his hands, he is shivering slightly. He turns back the bedclothes.

GEOFFREY's VOICE: But the next morning I knew it was hopeless. I had a temperature of a hundred and three and I had no alternative but to sweat it out.

CUT TO: A GIRL on a Switchboard at a Private Telephone Exchange.

An incoming call is registered.

GIRL: Anglo-British Chemical Corporation …

GEOFFREY: (*On the phone; he sounds weak and tired*) Can I speak to Mr Draper, please?

GIRL: Who is it calling?

GEOFFREY: Geoffrey Ryder …

GIRL: Oh, yes, Mr Ryder! One moment, please …

The GIRL transfers the call on the switchboard.

CUT TO: DENIS DRAPER on the telephone.
He is an important, precise, unfriendly little man.

DRAPER: (*On the phone*) Hello …?

GEOFFREY: Mr … Draper …?

DRAPER: Yes …

GEOFFREY: This is Geoffrey Ryder. I believe we have an appointment this afternoon for …

DRAPER: That's right. Four o'clock.

GEOFFREY: I'm awfully sorry, Mr Draper – I'm afraid I can't make it, I … I've got a touch of malaria …

DRAPER: (*Surprised*) Oh … Are you subject to that sort of thing?

GEOFFREY: Well – not exactly, but … Perhaps we could meet one day next week?

DRAPER: Next week's difficult – terribly difficult. Suppose you ring me on Thursday morning?

GEOFFREY: Yes, I'll … try and do … that …

DRAPER: All right, Mr Ryder. I hope you'll feel better by then.

DRAPER replaces the telephone.

CUT TO: The Exterior of the Flat. Knightsbridge.

GEOFFREY's VOICE: But I didn't feel better by Thursday morning. It wasn't until Wednesday of the following week that I really began to feel myself again. It was on a Wednesday afternoon that I went for a walk.

GEOFFREY comes out of the flat. He is wearing an overcoat and looks pale and tired. He is carrying a walking stick.

CUT TO: Outside Hyde Park.

GEOFFREY is strolling towards an entrance into Hyde Park. An open sports car – Hillman Minx – is parked by the kerb. The girl driver is studying a map; a small wire haired terrier by her side. GEOFFREY glances at the car but takes very little notice of it. GEOFFREY enters the park. The sports car drives slowly past him. The girl's head is turned away from GEOFFREY.

CUT TO: Hyde Park.

GEOFFREY is strolling along. He walks past the car which is parked near a large tree. He is deep in thought and takes no notice of either the car, the girl, or the dog. We do not see the girl's face very clearly; she is playing with the dog. GEOFFREY walks past and then it becomes obvious that the girl is watching GEOFFREY and we recognise her. It is STELLA.

CUT TO: Hyde Park.

GEOFFREY is still in the park, standing on a path, waving his stick at a passing taxi.

GEOFFREY's VOICE: It wasn't long before I began to feel tired, so I picked up a taxi and told the driver to take me back to the flat. Just as I was getting into the taxi a girl drove past in an open sports car. I'd seen her before somewhere but couldn't place her. Then suddenly I remembered. It was the girl with the camera.

The cab draws up and GEOFFREY opens the door and turns towards the driver. The sports car races past the taxi and as it does so GEOFFREY looks up and catches a glimpse of the girl. For a moment he is puzzled; realising that he has seen her before, but not sure where. Suddenly he remembers …

CUT TO: The Flat. The Living Room.
GEOFFREY enters from his walk; he takes off his overcoat and puts his stick down on a chair, then crosses to the drinks cabinet and thoughtfully mixes himself a drink. He crosses and puts his hand on the telephone but doesn't lift the receiver.

GEOFFREY's VOICE: I just didn't know whether to telephone the Inspector or not. I was sure I hadn't been mistaken about the girl, and yet in my present condition, the chances were he just wouldn't believe me. Also, to be frank, I was worried. If it was the girl, then was it a coincidence that I'd seen her in the Park – or was she in fact following me?

After a moment, GEOFFREY turns away from the telephone and lights a cigarette. He is obviously puzzled and a shade worried. He strolls back to the cabinet and adds more whisky to his drink. He stands with his back to the cabinet staring down at the glass; his thoughts on the girl and the recent turn of events.

The doorbell rings. GEOFFREY looks up from his glass; he is obviously surprised. He puts the glass down on the cabinet and crosses towards the door.

CUT TO: The Flat. The Front Door.
GEOFFREY opens the front door. DAVID WELDON is standing in the doorway. He is well-dressed and looks vaguely like an artistic diplomat. He is in his early fifties; wears a dark suit, a bowler hat perched forward, and carries

56

a rolled umbrella. There is a carnation in his buttonhole and
a silk handkerchief up his sleeve.

WELDON: Geoffrey Ryder?
GEOFFREY: Yes?
WELDON: (*Smiling*) Hello …
GEOFFREY: (*Puzzled*) Hello …
WELDON: It's David Weldon. We had a little chat on the telephone – remember?
GEOFFREY: Oh, yes!
WELDON: May I come in?
GEOFFREY: Why – yes, yes, of course.
WELDON: Jolly good …

CUT TO: The Flat. The Living Room.
GEOFFREY enters followed by DAVID WELDON.
WELDON: I hope I'm not barging in on anything?
GEOFFREY: No, I – I was just having a drink. (*He hesitates, then:*) Will you join me?
WELDON: Thank you, no. It's a little too early for me.
WELDON is slowly looking round the flat.
GEOFFREY: It's a little too early for me, too, but I haven't been feeling well and I thought perhaps … (*His words fade away; he is watching Weldon*) Are you looking for something?
WELDON: (*Hardly taking any notice of GEOFFREY*) Yes … (*Suddenly, turning*) I beg your pardon! (*Smiling at GEOFFREY*) My brother-in-law, Walter Smedley, borrowed a book of mine and I'd rather like it back because – I want to lend it to someone else.
GEOFFREY: Well, have a look round – see if you can find it.
WELDON: Thanks.

WELDON strolls round the room, looking at various books.
He seems to have plenty of time; he is quite unperturbed.

WELDON: My wife tells me you spent quite a pleasant
            evening together.
GEOFFREY: Yes, we – did.
WELDON: Where did you go – Chez Rousseau?
GEOFFREY: Yes.
WELDON: Thought so. Favourite spot of Kate's. Can't
            imagine why. (*He smiles at GEOFFREY;*
            very pleasant) It was very nice of you to take
            my wife out.
GEOFFREY: Not at all.
WELDON: (*Still looking round the room*) She can be
            jolly good fun. Lovely sense of humour. (*He*
            looks up) Impossible to live with though.
GEOFFREY: I wouldn't know about that.
WELDON: (*Seriously*) No. No, I don't suppose you
            would. (*He peers at the book on top of the*
            desk; takes out a pair of horn-rimmed glances
            and holds them to his eyes for a moment)
            Breakfast was the trouble …
GEOFFREY: (*Puzzled*) Breakfast?
WELDON: Yes. (*He puts his glasses back in his pocket*)
            Devilishly morose, deliberately hid The
            Times …
GEOFFREY: I'm sorry, I …
WELDON: (*Looking up from the books*) Katherine.
GEOFFREY: Oh. Oh, I see what you mean.
WELDON: (*A gesture round the room*) 'Fraid it's not in
            here.
GEOFFREY: There's some more books in the bedroom.
WELDON: (*Nodding towards the bedroom door*) May I?
GEOFFREY: Yes, of course.
WELDON: Jolly good …

58

WELDON goes into the bedroom. GEOFFREY stares after him; puzzled and a shade amused. He sits on the arm of the chair, holding his drink, looking towards the bedroom. After a moment, Weldon returns carrying a book.

GEOFFREY: I see you've found it.

WELDON: (*Crossing to GEOFFREY*) Yes. It was by the side of the bed. (*Holding up the book*) Have you read it?

GEOFFREY: (*Leaning forward*) The Revolution of …

WELDON: … Diplomatic Method …

GEOFFREY: (*Shaking his head*) No.

WELDON: You should. It's fascinating.

GEOFFREY: I shouldn't have thought it was your brother-in-law's cup of tea.

WELDON: No? Probably not. Still, you can never tell with Walter. Curious bird. I gather you met in Paris?

GEOFFREY: Yes.

WELDON: Jolly good place to meet.

There is a slight pause. Weldon stands, smiling at GEOFFREY.

GEOFFREY: (*More or less for something to say*) Well, I'm glad you found your book.

WELDON: Yes.

GEOFFREY: (*After a moment*) Is Kath – Mrs Weldon still in Scotland?

WELDON: Yes, I think she's due back on Wednesday. Incidentally, if you'd like to take her out again, don't hesitate, old man.

GEOFFREY: I won't.

WELDON: Just you go ahead …

GEOFFREY: Thank you very much.

WELDON: Kate and I are very good friends but we're not – well, I daresay she told you.

59

GEOFFREY:	She said you weren't living together, if that's what you mean.
WELDON:	That's what I mean, old boy. (*Suddenly*) Are you in the same line as Walter?
GEOFFREY:	No – I'm a metallurgical chemist.
WELDON:	Oh. Do you work in London?
GEOFFREY:	I'm hoping to.
WELDON:	What does that mean, exactly?
GEOFFREY:	It means I'm looking for a job.
WELDON:	(*Opening the book and looking down at it*) Isn't that rather a nuisance?
GEOFFREY:	(*Faintly irritated*) It's a necessity so far as I'm concerned.
WELDON:	(*Glancing up; his thought's elsewhere*) Yes … Yes, of course.
GEOFFREY:	I gather you've never had to work for a living, Mr Weldon.
WELDON:	No. (*Shaking his head; completely matter of fact*) No, I haven't. (*He looks down at the book; then looks up again and smiles at GEOFFREY*) I say, this is frightfully good, isn't it? (*Reading from the book*) "'Gullibility' as Sir Edward Grey once said to me, 'is in diplomacy a defect infinitely preferable to distrust'". (*He looks up from the book*) You know that doesn't only apply to diplomacy, does it? It applies to life. Let's face it, some of the most gullible people are the most likeable. I had an uncle once who … (*Stops; closes the book and smiles*) Oh, I'm so sorry. Obviously, you're not very interested in my uncle.
GEOFFREY:	No, but I'm interested in your brother-in-law.
WELDON:	My brother-in-law? Oh, you mean Walter?

GEOFFREY: Yes. What kind of man is Walter Smedley?

WELDON: But you met him! Damn it all, you wouldn't be here if you hadn't!

GEOFFREY: Yes, but I really know very little about him.

WELDON: So do I. So does Kate. We really all know very little about each other, if it comes to that. You remember what Lord Leighton said: "… there is always that other strange second man in me …"

GEOFFREY: (*Quietly*) You haven't answered my question.

WELDON: No? I thought I'd answered it rather well.

GEOFFREY: How often did you see Smedley?

WELDON: Oh, about once a month. We used to play billiards together; he was very good. Do you play billiards, Mr Ryder?

GEOFFREY: (*Ignoring the question*) Did Smedley ever say anything to you about a trip to Rome?

WELDON: (*Puzzled*) Rome?

GEOFFREY: Yes.

WELDON: (*Shaking his heads*) No. Was he going to Rome? I thought it was Genoa?

GEOFFREY: (*Nodding*) Yes, it was Genoa.

WELDON: Thought so. (*He consults his pocket watch*) Well, I must be off. (*A sudden thought*) Oh, by the way – Kate tells me you don't know many people in town …

GEOFFREY: No, I'm afraid I don't. I've got one or two letters to various people, but –

WELDON: Well, if you get too lonely, old man, just give me a ring. We'll have a spot of dinner one night?

GEOFFREY: That's very kind of you.

WELDON: I'm in the phone book. (*He crosses to the door then suddenly stops*) I say, just a minute!

	(*Turning back towards GEOFFREY*) Did you say you were a metallurgical chemist?
GEOFFREY:	Yes.
WELDON:	Does that mean you know all about (*To be completed*) and (*To be completed*) and mess about with (*To be completed*)

(FD note: The above lines need to be completed – technical research needs to be done.)

GEOFFREY:	(*Amused*) Roughly speaking.
WELDON:	Then, by George, you're just the man I'm looking for! You must come to dinner tomorrow night!
GEOFFREY:	I'm afraid tomorrow isn't possible. I haven't been very well during the past …
WELDON:	Nonsense! You'll be perfectly all right tomorrow. Good heavens, why didn't I think of this before? Old Elroyd'll be delighted to meet you. You're just his cup of tea.

GEOFFREY stares at WELDON; obviously surprised.

GEOFFREY:	Elroyd?
WELDON:	Yes.
GEOFFREY:	You don't mean Dr Charles Elroyd?
WELDON:	That's right. Do you know him?
GEOFFREY:	No, but – he's the head of Stanfield, the Government Research Laboratory …
WELDON:	That's the chap. He's been experimenting with (*To be researched*)
GEOFFREY:	(*Amused; correcting WELDON*) (*Reply to be researched*)
WELDON:	What do you call it?
GEOFFREY:	(*Reply to be researched*)
WELDON:	That's it. I don't know how the Dickens you people remember such names.
GEOFFREY:	But – is Dr Elroyd a friend of yours?

WELDON: We're both members of the same club, got
             absolutely nothing in common and yet always
             seem to get on like a house on fire. Anyway,
             about a month ago, I invited him to dinner;
             he's coming tomorrow night. (*He prods
             GEOFFREY with his umbrella*) And so are
             you, my friend.

GEOFFREY: Well – I must confess I'd certainly like to
             meet Dr Elroyd. (*Laughing*) If only to ask
             him why he didn't reply to my letter!

WELDON: Ninety-seven A, Mount Street. Seven-thirty –
             and don't dress.

WELDON crosses to the door.

GEOFFREY: (*Delighted*) Thank you very much, Mr
             Weldon. It's very kind of you, I shall look
             forward to it.

WELDON: Jolly good …

*WELDON turns, smiles at GEOFFREY; leans on his
umbrella. He looks very contented.*

CUT TO: The Flat. The Bathroom.
*GEOFFREY enters looking tired and drawn and opens the
bathroom cabinet above the wash basin. He takes out a bottle
of tablets and a drinking mug; he puts two or three tablets in
his mouth and pours himself a drink of water.*

GEOFFREY's VOICE: On Thursday afternoon, I had a
                   slight relapse, but I dosed myself
                   pretty heavily and was able to check
                   the fever. I was determined, at all
                   costs, to meet Dr Elroyd.

CUT TO: Billiard Balls on a Billiard Table.
*The red ball is facing a pocket and is obviously an easy pot.
A billiard cue is about to hit the spot ball towards the red.*

63

The camera follows the ball across the table, the spot misses the red and goes straight into the pocket.

GEOFFREY's VOICE: Elroyd was rather different from what I expected. For one thing he was much younger, and he had quite a keen sense of humour. He looked more like a successful author than a scientist. Also, although I wouldn't have believed it possible, his billiards was worse than mine.

ELROYD's VOICE: Now if only I could do that on the golf course!

The camera tracks back to reveal GEOFFREY, DAVID WELDON and DR CHARLES ELROYD who are all laughing.

GEOFFREY: That's game isn't it?

ELROYD is a rather pleasant, rotund, bookish looking man in the late forties. He wears a spotted bow tie and is smoking a pipe. His jacket hangs over the back of a chair.

WELDON: (*Amused*) It certainly is! I've played with some pretty shocking players in my time, but you two really strike a new low.

GEOFFREY is standing near the table, holding his jacket – he was about to put it on when ELROYD played his shot. WELDON wears a very fancy waistcoat.

ELROYD: (*Brushing his hand across the cloth*) I thought we did rather well, there isn't a ripple anywhere.

They are in a cosy room; panelled in oak and comfortably furnished. There are several armchairs, tables with decanters, syphon etc.

GEOFFREY: (*Putting on his jacket*) Well, you know what they say about this game. Sign of an ill spent youth …

WELDON: That's nonsense! The best player I ever struck was a diplomat – he died from overwork.

ELROYD: Really? A diplomat? What an extraordinary phenomena.

There is a knock on the door and MARY, a uniformed maid, enters.

MARY: (*To WELDON*) Excuse me, sir – you're wanted on the telephone.

WELDON: Who is it, Mary?

MARY: It's a personal call, sir.

WELDON: (*Nodding*) Yes, all right …

Exit MARY.

WELDON: (*To ELROYD and GEOFFREY*) Will you excuse me? I shan't be a moment. (*He crosses to the door*) Help yourself to drinks.

WELDON goes out. ELROYD crosses to the drinks table.

ELROYD: Would you like a whisky and soda?

GEOFFREY: Thank you, sir.

ELROYD: (*Preparing the drink*) Our host tells me you've been out in West Africa, Mr Ryder.

GEOFFREY: Yes, I was with the West African Chemical Company.

ELROYD: (*Looking up*) Indeed?

GEOFFREY: Wasn't Talbot-Naylor an old friend of yours, sir?

ELROYD: Yes, he was. (*Handing GEOFFREY his drink*) Do you know Talbot?

GEOFFREY: He joined us last year, only for six months though. We were experimenting with a new atomising plant, and he flew over from Cape Town. He only intended to stay a couple of days.

ELROYD: He's a funny old devil, but as wise as an owl.

GEOFFREY: I thought his book was very good.

ELROYD: Which one was that, the one on the pyrometturgical process?

GEOFFREY: No, that was the first one: I mean the handbook …

ELROYD: On Powder Metallurgy?

GEOFFREY: Yes.

ELROYD: Are you interested in Powder Metallurgy?

GEOFFREY: I've been specialising in it for two years; that's why I went out to the Gold Coast.

ELROYD: (*Looking at RYDER over the top of his glass*) You know, now I come to think of it, I seem to remember your name, Mr Ryder. Didn't you write me a letter or something?

GEOFFREY: A letter …

ELROYD: Yes, of course, that's right! You applied for a job. You wanted to work at Stanfield.

GEOFFREY: I still do.

ELROYD: Why?

GEOFFREY: Because I'm interested in what you're doing.

ELROYD: Aren't you interested in making money?

GEOFFREY: Of course.

ELROYD: Well, you won't make it at Stanfield. You'll work twelve hours a day for fifteen hundred a year – and no perks.

GEOFFREY: No perks?

ELROYD: (*Smiling*) Well –

GEOFFREY laughs.

ELROYD: You say you've been specialising?

GEOFFREY: Yes. I developed a new moulding process, rather on the lines of the Baxterdale Press.

ELROYD: Was it a success?

GEOFFREY: No …

ELROYD: Is that why you came home?

GEOFFREY: No, I thought it was about time I made a change. The climate was getting me down. I had malaria several times.

ELROYD: I see. (*A moment*) Have you done any work on condensation?

GEOFFREY: A little; chiefly from metallic carbonyls.

ELROYD: (*Interested*) Really? Was that with the West African Company?

GEOFFREY: No, that was before I went out there. I was with a firm called Stanley Brighouse.

ELROYD: At Liverpool?

GEOFFREY: That's right.

ELROYD: (*After a momentary hesitation*) We've been working on a new moulding process at Stanfield.

GEOFFREY: Yes, so I've heard.

ELROYD: (*A shade too casual*) It's based on the old Paradoil Hydraulic system.

GEOFFREY: (*Shaking his head*) That's not what I heard.

ELROYD looks at GEOFFREY.

ELROYD: No?

GEOFFREY: No. I heard you'd invented a new die and if it withstood the pressure, you'd get up to a hundred tons per square inch.

ELROYD: If it withstood the pressure! (*Laughing*) If pigs had wings, they could fly, Mr Ryder!

GEOFFREY: (*Smiling*) Not necessarily, Mr Elroyd.

ELROYD: (*Suddenly*) How much did they pay you – the African people?

GEOFFREY: Oh, dear!

ELROYD: What's the matter?

GEOFFREY: (*Thoughtfully*) I can't remember what I put in my letter.

ELROYD laughs.

ELROYD:	Was it more than fifteen hundred a year?
GEOFFREY:	Yes …
ELROYD:	(*Nodding*) M'm. (*He takes a cigar from his breast pocket*) Did I reply to your letter, Mr Ryder?
GEOFFREY:	No.
ELROYD:	I thought not. It's a curious trait. I never reply to letters that impress me.
GEOFFREY:	You must have a very large filing cabinet.
ELROYD:	(*Laughing*) Yes, I have. (*Preparing his cigar*) Where were you born?
GEOFFREY:	(*Puzzled*) In Wellington, New Zealand.
RYDER:	When?
GEOFFREY:	Nineteen twelve …
ELROYD:	Are you a bachelor?
GEOFFREY:	Yes.
ELROYD:	What are your politics?
GEOFFREY:	Politics!
ELROYD:	Yes.
GEOFFREY:	(*Contemptuously*) I don't bother with politics, I'm a metallurgical chemist not a politician.
ELROYD:	You read the newspapers; you must have some political bias.
GEOFFREY:	Well, now, it depends …
ELROYD:	On the paper?
GEOFFREY:	No, on when I read it. At breakfast I'm always violently Left, and at lunch violently Right.
ELROYD:	And at dinner?
GEOFFREY:	I invariably read a book.
ELROYD:	The reason I ask is, if by any chance you did come to Stanfield …
GEOFFREY:	Yes.
ELROYD:	You'd have to be screened.

GEOFFREY: Screened?

ELROYD: Yes.

GEOFFREY: I thought that sort of thing only happened in the Pictures?

ELROYD: (*Amused*) I don't mean 'grilling', Mr Ryder.

GEOFFREY: Well, what do you mean?

ELROYD: You'd be asked rather a lot of questions by a man called Alan Quinton – he's attached to M.I.5.

GEOFFREY: What sort of questions? What School did my father go to? Did I ever fall in love with the Art Mistress?

ELROYD: I think it's the Housemaster they're chiefly worried about. (*He lights his cigar; after a moment, when it's drawing satisfactorily*) Of course, speaking as a Scientist, there's one tremendous drawback, working at Stanfield.

GEOFFREY: Really? What's that?

ELROYD: (*Smiling at GEOFFREY*) You have to eat in the Canteen.

GEOFFREY laughs. DAVID WELDON returns.

WELDON: Well, do you think you chaps could do better at snooker?

GEOFFREY: We can try …

ELROYD joins WELDON near the billiard table.

ELROYD: Curiously enough, I've never played snooker.

WELDON: (*Extremely dubious*) Oh …

ELROYD: I suppose the principle's the same?

WELDON turns to get his snooker balls and his cue.

WELDON: Well, you've got to hit the balls, if that's what you mean.

ELROYD: (*Pulling WELDON's leg*) Yes, but aren't there more of them?

WELDON looks across at ELROYD; cocks his eyebrow at him.

CUT TO: The Flat. The Living Room. The following afternoon.

GEOFFREY is sitting at the desk, writing a letter. He is definitely unwell; his movements are tired and listless. He finishes the letter, takes out his diary and copies the address from the diary, then seals the envelope and sticks two twopenny stamps on it. He then rises and crosses into the bedroom, returning a few moments later with his hat and coat. He has left his diary on top of the bureau.

GEOFFREY's VOICE: I was delighted with my meeting with Dr Elroyd and the following afternoon, although I obviously had a temperature, I wrote a letter to Walter Smedley. I told him about meeting his sister, about Weldon, about Elroyd, and of course about the intruder. Since nothing had been stolen however I made light of the incident, I just didn't think there was any point in worrying him. When I'd finished the letter, I decided to take it down to the post box. I thought perhaps a breath of fresh air might make me feel better ...

GEOFFREY crosses towards the front door and as he does so the telephone rings. He returns to the centre of the room and lifts the receiver.

GEOFFREY: (*On the phone*) Hello?

ELROYD: (*On the other end; quite friendly*) Mr Ryder?

GEOFFREY: Yes ...

ELROYD: This is Dr Elroyd …

GEOFFREY: (*Pleasantly surprised*) Oh, good afternoon, doctor.

ELROYD: I'm sorry if I've disturbed you.

GEOFFREY: Not at all, sir.

ELROYD: Ryder, curiously enough, since I spoke to you last night one of my staff – a man called Kember – has been offered a post with the Pendleton Laboratory of California.

GEOFFREY: Indeed, sir?

ELROYD: Kember's married to an American girl and although he says he doesn't want to leave us I think he's pretty keen on the proposition. The point is – and mark you this is just a tentative suggestion – would you be interested in Kember's job if he accepts the American offer?

GEOFFREY: (*Delighted*) Why, yes – yes, I would …

ELROYD: Kember's what we call D2, Special Grade, which means he's getting about seventeen hundred a year.

GEOFFREY: When would you definitely know – about Kember, I mean?

ELROYD: Probably not for two or three weeks. In any case, I'm off to the Continent tomorrow. I shan't be back for at least ten days.

GEOFFREY: I see.

ELROYD: Think about it. There's no desperate hurry, but I thought I'd give you a ring.

GEOFFREY: I've already thought about it, sir – if I'm offered the job, I shall take it.

ELROYD: Good. Then we know where we are … I'll phone you the moment I get back.

GEOFFREY: Thank you, sir. And have a good holiday.

ELROYD: I'll try.

GEOFFREY: Where are you off to, the South of France?

ELROYD: Good heavens, no! That's not my cup of tea, Ryder! I'm going to a little place in Italy. Tolero.

GEOFFREY: (*Softly; astonished*) Tolero!

ELROYD: Yes; I don't suppose you've even heard of it. It's about twenty minutes from Rome.

ELROYD replaces the receiver. GEOFFREY looks tense and feverish, obviously staggered by ELROYD's words.

CUT TO: The exterior of the flat.   Knightsbridge. Afternoon.

GEOFFREY comes out of the flat wearing an overcoat and hat and using a walking stick. He is carrying the letter; his manner is deliberate and introspective.

GEOFFREY's VOICE: Tolero … Twenty minutes from Rome. I just couldn't believe it. And yet, I knew I'd heard correctly … I knew it wasn't my imagination … I knew that Dr Elroyd had actually said those words. All the way to the letter box I could hear his voice …

ELROYD's VOICE: (*Rising to crescendo*) Good heaven's no! That's not my cup of tea! I'm going to a little place   in Italy … Don't suppose you've even heard of it. It's about twenty minutes from Rome. Twenty minutes from Rome … Twenty minutes from Rome, Ryder!

CUT TO: A letter box on the corner of a busy Knightsbridge thoroughfare.

GEOFFREY approaches the letter box; posts the letter he is carrying, leans for a moment against the box, then commences to retrace his steps back to the flat. After a moment, he stops and puts his hand to his head; he sways slightly, then puts his hand out, as if to try to support himself. Several passers-by glance in GEOFFREY's direction, obviously puzzled by his behaviour. GEOFFREY continues along the pavement, then suddenly stops dead; he tries to continue, sways and finally collapses. Several passers-by rush to his assistance.

CUT TO: A modern, streamlined London County Council ambulance rushing down a busy West End thoroughfare towards Knightsbridge.

CUT TO: A Public Ward of a Hospital.

GEOFFREY is in a partly screened hospital bed. He is obviously very ill with malaria. SISTER DAWSON and a white coated DOCTOR are standing by the bed, examining the temperature chart. They look very concerned.

CUT TO: *GEOFFREY in bed; tossing and turning, in the grip of the malaria fever. The DOCTOR and another SISTER are watching him. A second doctor – DR STEVENS – is about to give GEOFFREY an injection.*

CUT TO: The Hospital Bed.

GEOFFREY is awake and although he is obviously still very ill, he has passed the crisis. DR STEVENS appears by the side of the bed.

GEOFFREY: What – what day is it?

STEVENS: Sunday …

GEOFFREY: How … long … have I been here …?

STEVENS: (*Feeling GEOFFREY's pulse*) Eight days. Do you feel better?

GEOFFREY nods and forces a smile. A UNIFORMED NURSE appears carrying a tray with a jar containing a thermometer.

CUT TO: A Private Office at the Hospital. Sunday afternoon.

SISTER DAWSON enters carrying a copy of a Sunday newspaper. She puts the newspaper down on the desk and commences to tidy the litter of X-ray photographs, letters, telephone directories, books, etc. DR STEVENS enters; he is carrying a stethoscope and wears a white coat.

STEVENS: Sister, I think Mr Wainwright is going to surprise us …

SISTER: No!

STEVENS: Yes … Definitely, yes!

SISTER: But he's 94 on Tuesday!

STEVENS: He might be 94, but he's getting better. The M.O. gave him penicillin this morning, and do you know what the old boy said?

SISTER: (*Smiling*) No …

STEVENS: He said – "I don't want any of that new-fangled muck, just get me a mild and bitter".

SISTER: (*Laughing*) What did the M.O. say?

STEVENS: If it hadn't been for the restraining influence of Matron, I think he'd have carried the old boy down to the Hare and Hounds.

SISTER DAWSON laughs and collects several of the X-ray plates.

STEVENS: (*Looking at his diary*) I see Mr Ryder's leaving us this afternoon …

SISTER: (*Nodding*) Yes, he wants to see you.

74

STEVENS: (*Looking at his watch*) I haven't a lot of time. I'm supposed to be relieving Hooper at half past three.

SISTER DAWSON nods and goes out. STEVENS sits at the desk and writes out a prescription. There is a knock on the door and GEOFFREY enters. He is carrying his hat and coat and walking stick. STEVENS rises from the desk with the prescription in his hand.

STEVENS: Well, Ryder – how do you feel?

GEOFFREY: Very much better, thanks to you, doctor.

STEVENS: (*Nodding*) You certainly look better. I've written you a prescription. Take this stuff for ten days, then I'll see you again.

GEOFFREY: Here – at the hospital?

STEVENS: Yes, I shall probably want a blood test. Phone me at the end of the week and we'll fix an appointment.

GEOFFREY moves nearer the desk and takes the prescription from DR STEVENS.

GEOFFREY: Thank you, doctor.

GEOFFREY glances down at the newspaper on the desk.

STEVENS: Now take it easy, Ryder – and remember what I told you yesterday afternoon. We know that complications do occur in malarial conditions but …

DR STEVENS notices GEOFFREY's expression. GEOFFREY is staring at the newspaper front page which has a photograph of DR ELROYD on it.

STEVENS: Is anything the matter?

GEOFFREY looks towards STEVENS. He is obviously astonished and bewildered.

GEOFFREY: When did this happen?

STEVENS: (*Puzzled*) What?

GEOFFREY: (*Holding out the newspaper*) This business with Dr Elroyd?

STEVENS: Oh, about four or five days ago. The papers have been full of it.

GEOFFREY: (*Unable to control his excitement; staring at the paper*) But – but what happened? It says here he was kidnapped …

STEVENS: (*A shrug*) Some papers say he was kidnapped, others say he deliberately walked out on us …

GEOFFREY: (*Astonished*) But – but that's ridiculous! Elroyd wouldn't do a thing like that!

STEVENS: How do you know he wouldn't? Quite a few of those scientific johnnies have done that sort of thing.

GEOFFREY: (*Still bewildered*) Yes, but – I knew Dr Elroyd …

STEVENS: A lot of people knew Pontecorvo; and judging from the number of newspaper articles a devil of a lot of people knew Burgess and MacLean!

GEOFFREY: (*Indicating the newspaper; still unable to control his excitement*) Yes, I know, but – Look, this is just a photograph, they take it for granted you know the story … What happened?

STEVENS: No one knows what happened. Apparently Elroyd went abroad and just didn't return …

GEOFFREY: Well, perhaps he's been taken ill …

STEVENS: Well, if he's been taken ill – where is he? He must be somewhere.

GEOFFREY sinks down into a chair facing the desk.

STEVENS: (*Watching GEOFFREY*) Was Dr Elroyd a particular friend of yours?

GEOFFREY: (*Quietly*) No, but – he'd more or less promised me a job at Stanfield; I was banking on it …

STEVENS: Oh, that's pretty rotten luck.

There is a knock on the door and SISTER DAWSON enters.

STEVENS: (*Indicating the newspaper*) Well, I don't believe this kidnapping story; it's the usual stuff they dish out when one of these long-haired characters acts true to type. But what the devil were M.I.5 doing, that's what I'd like to know. (*To SISTER DAWSON*) Yes, Sister?

SISTER: Matron would like a word with you, doctor.

STEVENS: Yes, certainly. (*To GEOFFREY*) I'll be back in a moment.

STEVENS crosses to the door.

GEOFFREY: May I use your phone?

STEVENS: Yes, go ahead.

STEVENS goes out followed by SISTER DAWSON.

GEOFFREY rises, crosses to the desk, and picks up one of the London Telephone Directories. He turns the pages, eventually finds the page he wants and runs his finger down the list of names. We see his finger pointing to the entry:

WELDON, DAVID. 97a Mount Street, W.1. Mayfair 9643 …

CUT TO: *GEOFFREY dialling the number. He looks tense and worried. We hear the number ringing out at the other end; the ringing continues for some little time; there is obviously no reply. GEOFFREY slowly replaces the receiver. He has a sudden thought and commences feeling in his pockets for his diary – but the diary is not there. He eventually recalls that he left it on the writing bureau in the flat, the afternoon he wrote the letter to Walter Smedley.*

GEOFFREY's VOICE: It occurred to me that Katherine Weldon would be back in London and that she could probably put me in touch with her husband. Why I was so desperately anxious to contact Weldon, I don't know. It was just that, well – he'd introduced me to Elroyd and I thought it was possible – just possible – that he might have some inside information about him. I couldn't remember Katherine's number and I hadn't got my diary on me. I thought at first, I'd lost it, then I suddenly remembered I'd left it on the writing bureau the afternoon I wrote the letter to Walter Smedley.

CUT TO: The Flat. The Living Room. Later the same afternoon.

GEOFFREY enters waring his hat and coat and carrying his walking stick and several letters. He takes off his hat and coat; puts down his stick; crosses to the writing bureau; and picks up his diary. He looks up KATHERINE WELDON's telephone number in the diary and then crosses to the telephone and dials. Once again, we hear the number ringing out at the other end of the line. After a pause, the receiver is lifted, and we hear a boy's voice. CYRIL is about twelve or thirteen; a definite Cockney.

CYRIL: (*On the other end of the line*) 'Ello? … Oo is that?

GEOFFREY: (*On the phone*) Is that Putney 8044?

CYRIL: S'right …

GEOFFREY: Can I speak to Mrs Weldon, please?

CYRIL:	Missis who?
GEOFFREY:	Mrs Weldon …
CYRIL:	Oo do you want?
GEOFFREY:	(*Looking at his diary*) That is Putney 8044?
CYRIL:	S'right …
GEOFFREY:	Well, I want to speak to Mrs Weldon – Mrs Katherine Weldon.

There is a pause, then a muffled conversation can be heard on the other end of the line. GEOFFREY looks tense as he waits.

WOMAN:	What is it, Cyril?
CYRIL:	I don't know, Mum. I don't know what 'ees on about.
WOMAN:	Give it to me, love.
GEOFFREY:	(*Exasperated*) Hello?
WOMAN:	(*On the other end of the phone; tough and Cockney*) Now what is it? What's this all about?
GEOFFREY:	(*Politely; controlling himself*) Oh, good afternoon. I'm sorry to trouble you but I want to speak to Mrs Weldon …
WOMAN:	You've got the wrong number. This is Putney 8044 …
GEOFFREY:	Yes, I know that, that's why …
WOMAN:	There's no one 'ere called Weldon. The name's Duckworth …

The WOMAN replaces the receiver. GEOFFREY looks at the receiver he is holding, then thoughtfully replaces it; he looks at the diary then slowly puts it in his inside pocket. He takes out his cigarette case then changes his mind and replaces it. Puzzled, and obviously worried, he loosens his tie, crosses and picks up his hat and coat, and turns towards the bedroom.

CUT TO: The Flat. The Bedroom.

GEOFFREY enters and crosses towards the chest of drawers. He stops dead; his face registering horror and astonishment. GEOFFREY crosses to the bed. WALTER SMEDLEY is sprawled across the bed – dead. There is a revolver on the bedclothes near his left hand; his right hand is dangling over the side of the eiderdown and is clutching the gold cigarette-case. The cigarette case is open, and the contents can be seen; they are the Sleeper Reservation document, and the torn map from a guidebook.

GEOFFREY stares down at SMEDLEY; he moves as if to touch the revolver then suddenly checks himself. He looks down at the piece of paper and the map. He picks up the two documents and examines them. We see on the map of Rome, Tolero is clearly marked. The words "Twenty Minutes From Rome" are scribbled across the top of the page.

CUT TO: ALAN QUINTON's Office in Mayfair.

QUINTON is sitting behind his desk listening to GEOFFREY RYDER. INSPECTOR MANN is sitting in the chair opposite QUINTON.

GEOFFREY: They were the documents that the girl had photographed; the Sleeper reservation ticket, and the map. Obviously, they must have been in the cigarette case the whole time.

QUINTON: Go on, Mr Ryder.

GEOFFREY: After I'd examined the documents I sent for the police. I intended to tell the Inspector the whole story, then I suddenly remembered that Dr Elroyd had mentioned your name and that you were connected to M.I.5. I made up my mind to tell my story to you and no one else.

QUINTON: I see. (*A moment*) And that's the whole story, Mr Ryder?

GEOFFREY:	Yes.
MANN:	(*Quietly*) Not quite the whole story.
QUINTON:	(*Looking towards MANN*) No, Inspector?
MANN:	(*To GEOFFREY*) I think you know what I'm referring to, sir.
GEOFFREY:	(*To MANN*) Sunday afternoon … my going to Church?

INSPECTOR MANN nods. GEOFFREY gives a slight shrug.

MANN:	I still can't understand why you didn't tell me, sir.
GEOFFREY:	It didn't seem to me to be important.
MANN:	But you must have thought it was important – you know perfectly well that you had to establish an alibi.
GEOFFREY:	And you think that's why I went to Church, Inspector – to establish an alibi?
MANN:	No, sir, I'm not suggesting that.
GEOFFREY:	Then what are you suggesting?
MANN:	I'm suggesting that when I questioned you, you knew perfectly well that you'd been to Church, but you deliberately didn't tell me about it.
GEOFFREY:	(*With almost the suggestion of a smile*) Now why should I do that?
MANN:	(*Quite frankly; puzzled*) I don't know why, Mr Ryder.
QUINTON:	I'm sorry, Inspector, I don't quite follow this.
MANN:	Well, let me continue the story, sir. After Ryder discovered Smedley, he sent for the police. We arrived on the scene about twenty minutes later. That, approximately, a quarter past four. While I was talking to Mr Ryder the police doctor examined the body.

CUT TO: The Flat. The Bedroom.

DR ROSS, a Police Doctor, is examining the body of WALTER SMEDLEY. A Plain Clothes Man is taking photographs of the room and the bed. SERGEANT GORRINGE is present, watching the proceedings. A UNIFORMED POLICE OFFICER stands near the open bedroom door. DR ROSS completes his examination and turns away from the bed.

ROSS: (*To GORRINGE*) All right ... I've finished.

GORRINGE: (*To the UNIFORMED OFFICER*) Tell Baker ...

OFFICER: Yes, sir.

The UNIFORMED OFFICER goes out.

GORRINGE: Well, doctor?

ROSS: Where's the Inspector?

GORRINGE: He'll be here in a minute; he's in the lounge with Mr Ryder.

ROSS: (*Picking up his bag from off the bed*) Do me a favour, Sergeant.

GORRINGE: Yes, sir.

ROSS: If you ever commit a murder, don't do it at the weekend.

GORRINGE: I'll try to oblige, sir.

INSPECTOR MANN enters from the living room. His manner is slightly brusque.

MANN: (*To ROSS*) Well, doctor?

ROSS: The cause of death was (*To be researched*). The bullet penetrated the (*To be researched*) He died instantaneously.

(*FD note: The above lines need to be completed – technical research needs to be done.*)

MANN: When?

ROSS: It's difficult to say without an autopsy, but –

82

MANN: Spare me the autopsy routine, just give me a
             time. Unofficial, off the record.
ROSS: Well, at a rough guess, I should say not
             earlier than two o'clock and not later than
             four.
MANN: (*Nodding*) Right …
ROSS: (*Indicating SMEDLEY's wristlet watch*) That
             ties up with his watch, in case you're
             interested.
MANN: So you noticed the watch?
ROSS: Yes, but don't worry, it didn't influence me.
MANN: (*Speaking to SERGEANT GORRINGE, yet
             indicating SMEDLEY*) Have you finished,
             Sergeant?
GORRINGE: Yes, sir.
*The INSPECTOR stoops down and unstraps SMEDLEY's
wristlet watch. He looks at the watch. The glass is broken,
and it has stopped at approximately half past three.*
ROSS: (*Faintly patronising*) I remember reading a
             mystery story once, the whole plot revolved
             round the dead man's watch …
MANN: (*Dead expression*) No …
ROSS: (*Nodding*) There was a struggle … The
             murderer took the watch, turned it back an
             hour, and then deliberately smashed it.
             (*There is no reaction from the INSPECTOR*)
             It was to establish an alibi.
MANN: You surprise me.
*MANN looks at DR ROSS, then turns and walks out of the
bedroom.*

CUT TO: The Flat. The Living Room.

GEOFFREY is sitting on the arm of one of the armchairs. He looks worried; is smoking a cigarette. MANN enters from the bedroom; he is still holding the watch.

MANN: Mr Ryder, there are one or two points I want to get quite clear.

GEOFFREY: Yes, Inspector?

MANN: I take it, there's no doubt in your mind that the dead man is Walter Smedley?

GEOFFREY: He's the man I met in Paris; the man who lent me the flat – he called himself Walter Smedley.

MANN: (*Nodding*) I think you told me that you'd met his sister and brother-in-law … A Mr and Mrs David Weldon.

GEOFFREY: Yes, that's correct. His sister actually met me at the Airport.

MANN: Have you tried to contact Mr and Mrs Weldon – this afternoon, I mean?

GEOFFREY: Yes.

MANN: What happened?

GEOFFREY: I couldn't get a reply from Weldon's number and there appeared to be some confusion over the other one.

MANN: What was the other number?

GEOFFREY: Putney … 8044.

The INSPECTOR nods and looks down at the watch he is holding.

MANN: (*Thoughtfully*) What time was it when you left the hospital?

GEOFFREY: It was about five or ten minutes past three.

MANN: I think you said you walked part of the way and then picked up a cab.

GEOFFREY: (*With the faintest hesitation*) Yes.

MANN: (*Looking up*) How far did you walk?

GEOFFREY: About … a mile I should imagine.

MANN: Where were you exactly when you picked up the taxi?

GEOFFREY: (*Vaguely*) Oh, I forget.

MANN looks at GEOFFREY.

MANN: You forget, Mr Ryder?

GEOFFREY: I don't know London terribly well, Inspector. I imagine I wasn't very far from Oxford Street.

MANN: And the taxi brought you straight back to the flat?

GEOFFREY: Yes.

MANN: So you got to the flat at about –?

GEOFFREY: Exactly ten minutes to four.

MANN stares at GEOFFREY for a moment and then looks down at the watch; suddenly he puts the watch in his pocket and looks up again.

MANN: Thank you. (*He turns to go back into the bedroom*)

GEOFFREY: (*Suddenly*) Inspector …

MANN: (*Turning*) Yes, sir?

GEOFFREY: (*He hesitates, then:*) Do you happen to know a man called Quinton?

MANN: Quinton?

GEOFFREY: I understand he's attached to M.I.5.

MANN: (*Faintly surprised*) Yes, I've heard of Mr Quinton, sir. Why?

GEOFFREY: I may want to get in touch with him.

MANN: Oh, sir?

GEOFFREY: Would that be possible?

MANN: (*Slowly; puzzled*) Why, yes … I don't see why not.

MANN looks at GEOFFREY.

CUT TO: ALAN QUINTON's Office. As before.

MANN: I checked Mr Ryder's story with Dr Stevens. It was perfectly true. He was discharged from the hospital at approximately ten past three.

QUINTON: Go on, Inspector.

MANN: When I was leaving the hospital I noticed a taxi rank opposite the main gate, and it suddenly struck me as being rather odd that a comparatively sick man like Mr Ryder should choose to take a walk before picking up a cab; obviously he must have seen the rank the moment he walked out of the hospital.

QUINTON: Yes, but was there a cab on the rank at ten past three?

MANN turns and looks at GEOFFREY.

MANN: Yes, there was, sir. I had a word with the driver.

GEOFFREY looks impassive.

CUT TO: *HAROLD BOLTON, a typical Cockney taxi driver who is sitting in the driving seat of his cab, reading a Sunday newspaper. After a moment, MANN arrives, and HAROLD puts down the paper.*

MANN: Good afternoon …

HAROLD: 'Afternoon, Guv'nor … (*He turns to open the passenger door*)

MANN: (*Stopping HAROLD*) No, that's all right … (*He takes his wallet out of his pocket and shows it to HAROLD*)

HAROLD: (*Surprised*) Oh … Can I help you, Inspector?

MANN: Yes. What time did you come on duty this afternoon?

HAROLD: Be about 'alf past two, sir.

MANN: And you've been here the whole afternoon?

HAROLD:	No, sir – I 'ad a fare just after three. I got back here about a quarter past four.
MANN:	Who was the fare – one of your regulars?
HAROLD:	No – gent I've never seen before. He came out of the 'orspital.
MANN:	(*Interested*) At about ten past three?
HAROLD:	Yes, it would be about ten past.
MANN:	Describe him …
HAROLD:	(*Puzzled; scratching his head*) Well …
MANN:	Well, was he tall or short?
HAROLD:	About medium, I'd say.
MANN:	Clean shaven?
HAROLD:	Yes …
MANN:	Dark?
HAROLD:	Yes, I suppose you'd call 'im dark …
MANN:	How old?
HAROLD:	Ooh, fortyish. Quite good looking in his way …
MANN:	What was he wearing?
HAROLD:	Grey overcoat, dark suit, trilby … (*Suddenly*) Oh, and he 'ad a walking stick!
MANN:	(*Pleased; nodding*) Thank you. Now where did you take him to?
HAROLD:	(*Matter of fact*) To Church, sir.
MANN:	(*Astonished*) To Church?
HAROLD:	Yes, sir.
MANN:	Which Church?
HAROLD:	The one at the bottom of Frinton Road …
MANN:	(*Puzzled*) Did he go in the Church?
HAROLD:	Why, yes, of course. He stayed there abaht a quarter of an hour.
MANN:	Was there a service?
HAROLD:	Yes, there's one every Sunday at three o'clock …

MANN:	And you waited for him while he was in the Church?
HAROLD:	(*Puzzled*) Yes, he asked me to. When he came out, I took him to an address in Knightsbridge. Now what was it? Clarence … Clarington … Clarendon Mews, that's it …
MANN:	(*Quietly*) Number 2, Clarendon Mews …
HAROLD:	(*Nodding*) That's right – it was Number 2 …
MANN:	(*Quietly; yet with authority*) Now let's get this quite clear. He came out of the hospital at about ten minutes past three, you took him straight to the Church, he stayed there approximately a quarter of an hour and then you drove him to Number 2, Clarendon Mews.
HAROLD:	That's right.
MANN:	What time was it when you arrived at Clarendon Mews?
HAROLD:	Ten minutes to four.
MANN:	You're sure of that?
HAROLD:	I'm positive. I was back 'ere at four fifteen.
MANN:	(*Satisfied*) All right … Thank you very much. By the way, what's your name?
HAROLD:	I'll give you a card, Guv'nor.

HAROLD searches in the glove box for a card.

CUT TO: ALAN QUINTON's Office. As before.
GEOFFREY still looks impassive; apparently unaffected by INSPECTOR MANN's statement.

QUINTON:	Well, Mr Ryder?
GEOFFREY:	Forgive me, but I still don't see why the Inspector should attach importance to the fact that I went to Church.

QUINTON: It isn't the fact that you went to Church – it's the fact that you didn't tell the Inspector anything about it.

GEOFFREY: (*A shade angry*) But why should I?

QUINTON: Because this is a murder case and you're a possible suspect, you admitted that yourself.

GEOFFREY: But surely, so far as I am concerned, the only important factor is the time element, the time that I arrived back at the flat.

QUINTON: (*Nodding*) No one disputed the fact that you told the truth about the time, in any case the taxi driver confirms it. But you lied, quite deliberately, about your movements.

GEOFFREY looks at QUINTON for a moment and then rises; he crosses the room and stands with his back to the desk. After a little while he turns.

GEOFFREY: Yes, I did.

QUINTON: Why?

There is now a faint suggestion of agitation about GEOFFREY's manner and movements. INSPECTOR MANN is watching GEOFFREY.

MANN: Well, Mr Ryder?

GEOFFREY: (*After a moment*) When I came out of the hospital, I was worried and depressed. The news about Elroyd had upset me and I had an unhappy feeling that both Katherine and her husband were, in some way, mixed up in it. It's difficult for me to explain now how I felt. Apart from a feeling of intense loneliness, I was in a strange, self-pitying mood. Suddenly, quite out of the blue, I made up my mind to go to Church …

MANN: (*Quietly*) That seems to make sense, Mr Ryder – but why didn't you tell me?

89

GEOFFREY: (*Looking straight at the INSPECTOR*) Because I didn't think you'd believe me.

The INSPECTOR looks at GEOFFREY, then quietly nods his head.

There is a pause, then QUINTON speaks.

QUINTON: What made you pick that particular Church?

GEOFFREY: Well – I knew there was a service at three o'clock.

QUINTON: Had you been there before?

GEOFFREY: (*After a very faint, hardly perceptible, hesitation*) No, but I'd seen the notice board outside.

QUINTON: (*Enigmatically*) I see.

There is a knock on the door and RONALD FREED enters.

FREED: (*To QUINTON*) Excuse me, sir. (*Handing QUINTON an envelope*) This has just arrived.

QUINTON: Thank you. (*He looks up at GEOFFREY and the INSPECTOR*) Excuse me. (*He opens the envelope and takes out a single sheet of notepaper which he looks at; his expression remains unchanged*)

We see that the notepaper has a neat, embossed address: "Department I.S. Whitehall"

Underneath the address are typed the words: Urgent and Strictly Confidential. This is followed by a typewritten message and a signature, which is simply the initial "T" written in ink. The message reads:

"Am in complete agreement. Confide C.I.D. if necessary".

QUINTON: (*To FREED*) Has Miss Elliot returned?

FREED: Yes, sir. She's with Colonel Smith at the moment.

QUINTON nods to FREED, who turns and goes out. QUINTON rises from the desk.

QUINTON: (*To GEOFFREY and the INSPECTOR*) Will
              you excuse me? I just want a word with one
              of my colleagues.
MANN: (*Rising; looking at GEOFFREY*) Well, if Mr
              Ryder hasn't got anything else to add, sir,
              there's no reason why we shouldn't be
              making a move.
QUINTON: No, it's all right, Inspector. I shan't be a
              moment.
MANN: (*Sitting down again*) Very good, sir

QUINTON crosses to the door, watched by GEOFFREY.

CUT TO: A tape recording machine.

*Both the machine and the speaker are turned on. The tape
revolves and voices can be heard coming from the machine.
The camera tracks back to reveal STELLA and COLONEL
SMITH listenening to the recorder. They are in a small office;
the door of which is sound proofed. SMITH is about fifty-two
or three, wears a smart tweed suit and smokes a pipe. A
pleasant man.*

GEOFFREY's VOICE: (*From the recorder*) But for
                   goodness' sake be reasonable,
                   Smedley!
SMEDLEY's VOICE: (*Angrily*) I didn't come from Genoa
                   just to be reasonable …
GEOFFREY's VOICE: But I told you about the malaria. I
                   told you it was liable to happen …
SMEDLEY's VOICE: Then why didn't you contact us?
GEOFFREY's VOICE: How the hell could I? Don't you
                   realise I was delirious for three
                   days!
SMEDLEY's VOICE: Delirious! That must have been
                   interesting …

91

QUINTON enters the office, closing the padded doors behind him. He stands for a moment listening to the voices.

GEOFFREY's VOICE: (*Softly; tensely*) My God, I never thought of that!

SMEDLEY's VOICE: There seems to have been quite a lot of things you haven't thought of, Mr Ryder.

GEOFFREY's VOICE: Look, Smedley, I don't get this! You've got Elroyd so what the devil are you ...

SMEDLEY's VOICE: (*Interrupting GEOFFREY*) We haven't got Elroyd!

GEOFFREY's VOICE: (*Astonished*) You haven't?

SMEDLEY's VOICE: No ...

GEOFFREY's VOICE: (*Puzzled*) Then where is he?

SMEDLEY's VOICE: Exactly – where is he?

GEOFFREY's VOICE: (*A moment; nervously*) Smedley, this isn't going to make any difference, is it?

SMEDLEY's VOICE: What do you mean?

GEOFFREY's VOICE: You owe me five hundred pounds.

SMEDLEY's VOICE: You don't expect us to pay you when the deal didn't go through?

GEOFFREY's VOICE: That's not what you said in Paris ...

SMEDLEY's VOICE: Never mind what I said in Paris ...!

GEOFFREY's VOICE: (*Tensely*) Smedley, I need that five hundred ...

SMEDLEY's VOICE: You may need it, my friend, but ... (*He stops; quietly*) Put that thing away ... (*A shade frightened*) Ryder, don't be a fool, put it away ...

QUINTON nods to STELLA and she leans forward and switches off the machine.

92

QUINTON: (*To SMITH*) That seems satisfactory, George.

SMITH: Yes, perfect.

QUINTON: (*To STELLA*) Did you have any difficulty, Stella?

STELLA: No, it was easy this afternoon. (*Smiling*) I knew he wasn't going to walk in on me.

QUINTON: I hope you were careful.

STELLA: (*To QUINTON; putting her hand on the recorder*) Would you like to hear it from the beginning, sir?

QUINTON: No, later. (*To SMITH*) George, Ryder's still here, he'll be leaving in a few minutes with the Inspector.

SMITH: (*Nodding*) Yes …

QUINTON: I want you to get hold of the Inspector without Ryder knowing; I don't care how you do it – but do it.

SMITH: Right …

QUINTON: (*To STELLA*) What do they call the café on the Euston Road, the self-service place? I met you there last week.

STELLA: The Dutch Treat.

QUINTON: That's it. (*Nodding. To SMITH*) Tell the Inspector I'll see him there in forty-five minutes.

SMITH nods; sucks his pipe.

QUINTON: (*Handing SMITH the memo*) Read this, George, and then destroy it.

SMITH: Yes, sir.

QUINTON smiles at STELLA and goes out of the office. SMITH looks at the memo; takes a cigarette lighter out of his pocket; flicks his lighter and applies the flame to the piece of paper.

CUT TO: *DETECTIVE INSPECTOR MANN lighting a cigarette with his cigarette lighter.*

He is sitting at a wall-table in a corner of a self-service café. There is a tray in front of him containing the remains of a meal and a half full cup of coffee. He smokes his cigarette and looks thoughtful. After a moment, QUINTON arrives carrying a cup of coffee. He wears a bowler hat and carries a rolled umbrella over his arm.

QUINTON: (*Sitting down*) Sorry I'm late.

MANN: (*Turning*) That's all right, sir. (*He offers QUINTON the sugar*) Sugar?

QUINTON: Thank you. (*He helps himself to sugar and stirs his coffee*) Well – were you surprised to get my message?

MANN: Yes, I was.

QUINTON: I've just been having a talk to the Assistant Commissioner. He appears to think very highly of you, Inspector.

MANN: He might be prejudiced, sir.

QUINTON: Yes?

MANN: I married his niece.

QUINTON smiles and stirs his coffee.

A pause.

QUINTON: (*Quietly*) What do you make of Ryder?

MANN: (*Shaking his head*) I don't know. (*Seriously bewildered*) I just don't know …

QUINTON: Did you believe his story?

MANN: Yes, I did, except for the fact that … (*He hesitates, then:*) If he was telling the truth about that girl, the one that searched the flat, why did he take the film out of the camera? You'll never convince me it was just idle curiosity.

QUINTON: Go on, Inspector.

94

MANN: Even if you accept his explanation, I still
             don't understand why he didn't tell me about
             it after the negatives had been stolen.
QUINTON: Go on, Inspector …
MANN: Then there's all that business about going to
             Church I'm … not … sure about … that, sir.
QUINTON: (*Smiling*) I thought you were. I thought he'd
             convinced you.
MANN: He convinced me at the time, but – I've been
             thinking about it. If I was involved in a
             murder case and I'd been to Church the
             afternoon the murder was committed, I'd
             certainly tell the police about it. I'd make a
             point of it, in fact.
QUINTON: Yes, but you're not Mr Ryder.
MANN: (*Suddenly, turning towards QUINTON; quite
             friendly, yet definite*) Well, sir – what's your
             opinion of all this? You heard his story. Was
             he telling the truth?
QUINTON: (*After a moment, then:*) At times – yes.
MANN: And the rest –?
QUINTON: Was a fabrication.
*The INSPECTOR looks at QUINTON, then knocks the ash of
his cigarette onto the plate.*
MANN: (*Quietly, still looking at the plate*) That girl –
             the one that broke into the flat.
QUINTON: Yes?
MANN: Was she one of your people? (*He looks up at
             QUINTON*)
QUINTON: Yes, she was. Inspector, I want you to have
             another talk with the taxi driver; then go to
             the Church and get hold of the Padre; see if he
             remembers Ryder.

MANN:	(*Slowly*) You don't think perhaps Ryder had an appointment with someone – at the Church, I mean?
QUINTON:	It's a possibility, but I don't think so. (*He stirs his coffee*) It's obvious he didn't want you to trace the taxi, that's why he told you he went for a walk before picking it up.
MANN:	Yes.
QUINTON:	Nevertheless, he knew there was a chance that you would trace it, and in my opinion that's why he told the driver to take him to the Church.
MANN:	What do you mean, sir?
QUINTON:	He knew that if you ever caught up with the taxi, that's the one thing you'd concentrate on.
MANN:	In other words, his visit to the Church was a blind, to cover up something?
QUINTON:	(*Looking up at the INSPECTOR*) I think so …
MANN:	(*Thoughtfully*) I wonder if you're right about this …?
QUINTON:	How did Ryder know that that particular Church had a service on at three o'clock?
MANN:	He said he'd noticed it on the board.
QUINTON:	Which means he must have been in Frinton Road on a previous occasion.

The INSPECTOR looks at QUINTON; then rises and stubs out his cigarette on the plate.

MANN:	I get the point, Mr Quinton.
QUINTON:	I shall be back in my office by eight o'clock.

CUT TO: The Flat. The Living Room.
GEOFFREY enters wearing his outdoor clothes; he has just returned from his interview with QUINTON. He switches on

the main light, takes off his hat and coat and then crosses to the drinks cabinet and mixes himself a drink. He stands, glass in hand, deep in thought. He is fairly calm, and obviously not unduly worried. After a moment, he crosses to the table and opens the silver cigarette box and takes out a cigarette. As he holds the cigarette he stoops down and switches on the table lamp. The light does not come on. GEOFFREY looks at the lamp; takes out the bulb and examines it. The bulb is obviously unbroken; he returns it to the holder and then crosses to the bedroom.

CUT TO: The Flat. The Bedroom Door.
GEOFFREY enters and reaches out for the light switch. The light is not working in the bedroom. He hesitates in the open doorway; silhouetted by the light from the living room.

CUT TO: The Flat. A very large wall cupboard.
A beam of light on the cupboard door and we see that the cupboard is marked "Electricity: Fuses".
GEOFFREY is standing on a stool, or small ladder, holding a torch. He takes a spool of fuse wire out of his pocket and after studying it for a moment opens the cupboard door. The light from GEOFFREY's torch falls on the interior of the cupboard. It contains the usual fuse-boxes; electrical switches, etc, – but as the light from the torch is lowered, we can see that the cupboard also contains a small, compact, recording unit. GEOFFREY is startled and bewildered.

CUT TO: The Flat. The Bedroom.
The light is on. GEOFFREY rushes in from the living room. He takes the suitcase out from under the bed and starts to pack.

CUT TO: ALAN QUINTON's Office. Eight o'clock the same evening.

COLONEL SMITH is sitting at QUINTON's desk writing a report. The door opens and FREED enters; he carries a sheaf of papers.

SMITH: (*Looking up*) I thought you'd gone home.

FREED: No, sir. I've been working. Is Mr Quinton coming back tonight?

SMITH: Yes, he should be here any minute.

FREED: It's about the Italian cipher, sir. I think it ought to be changed.

SMITH: But we've just changed it.

FREED: Yes, I know.

SMITH: Well – what's the matter with it?

FREED: (*A shade embarrassed*) It's too easy, Colonel.

SMITH: Do you mean to say you've cracked it?

FREED nods.

SMITH: When?

FREED: This afternoon, sir – after tea.

SMITH: What do you do in your spare time, Freed – learn Greek?

FREED: I know Greek, sir.

The door opens and QUINTON enters. SMITH rises from the desk.

QUINTON: Hello, Freed! Are you on duty tonight?

FREED: Not officially, sir.

QUINTON: (*To FREED*) Well, I'm expecting Inspector Mann – send him in as soon as he arrives.

FREED: Yes, sir.

FREED puts the documents down on the desk and then goes out.

QUINTON: (*To SMITH*) It's all right, George – don't get up. (*He takes off his hat and coat*) I suppose there's no news?

SMITH:	About Weldon? (*QUINTON nods*) No, nothing …
QUINTON:	Well, Ryder's our only chance now, if he doesn't lead us to him, we've had it.
SMITH:	Always providing Ryder knows where he is.
QUINTON:	You don't think he does?
SMITH:	No, I don't. And there's another danger …
QUINTON:	What's that?
SMITH:	Supposing the police arrest him?
QUINTON:	Well?
SMITH:	As soon as they arrest him, he's out of circulation; he won't lead us anywhere.
QUINTON:	Yes, but if he's arrested, he may get really scared, in which case he'll talk. (*He looks at SMITH*) I'm not sure that isn't our best bet, George.

There is a knock on the door and INSPECTOR MANN enters. He looks faintly excited and rather pleased with himself.

QUINTON:	(*Turning*) Oh, hello, Inspector!
MANN:	Good evening, sir.
QUINTON:	I don't think you know Colonel Smith – a colleague of mine.

MANN crosses and shakes hands with SMITH.

SMITH:	Glad to know you, Inspector.
MANN:	How do you do, sir?
QUINTON:	Well – did you see the taxi driver?
MANN:	Yes, sir – and the Padre.
QUINTON:	Well?
MANN:	He went into the Church all right, he stayed there fifteen minutes. The Parson remembers him.
SMITH:	Was he alone?
MANN:	(*Smiling*) The whole time, sir.
QUINTON:	M'm.

MANN:	(*After a moment; significantly*) But he bought a newspaper, sir.
QUINTON:	(*Looking up*) When?
MANN:	Before he went into the Church. The cabby didn't think it was important …
QUINTON:	Was it important?
MANN:	(*Unable to restrain himself any longer*) I'll say!
QUINTON:	What do you mean?
MANN:	He went into a shop to buy it. You know the sort of place – newsagent-cum-tobacconist.
QUINTON:	Go on, Inspector.
MANN:	There's a glass case outside the front door; it's full of postcards. For half a crown a week you can advertise anything you want. (*He takes an envelope out of his inside pocket*) For instance, a gentleman lost his cigarette case. I copied the advertisement down. (*He reads from the envelope*) "Gold square cigarette case belonging to Italian gentleman lost near Knightsbridge; finder rewarded. Telephone before mid-day Western 3127".
QUINTON:	(*Taking the envelope from MANN*) What is Western 3127?
MANN:	The number doesn't exist; it's part of the message – the whole thing is obviously in code.
QUINTON:	(*Quickly; turning to SMITH*) Get Freed! (*To MANN*) Who inserted this?

SMITH speaks into the intercom system on the desk.

SMITH:	Freed, Mr Quinton wants you. Come up straight away.
MANN:	Smedley.
QUINTON:	How do you know it was Smedley?

100

MANN:	The newsagent described him …
QUINTON:	When did he place the advert?
MANN:	Nearly a fortnight ago.
SMITH:	While Ryder was in hospital?
MANN:	Yes.
SMITH:	(*To QUINTON*) You can see what happened. As soon as Ryder came out of the hospital, he went to the shop to see if there was a message for him.
QUINTON:	(*Irritated*) We ought to have spotted that wretched shop weeks ago!

There is a knock on the door and FREED enters.

QUINTON:	Freed, you remember the cable to Genoa about the cigarette case, the one Ryder sent?
FREED:	Yes, sir.
QUINTON:	(*Handing FREED the envelope*) I think this is the same code; get to work on it.
FREED:	(*Taking the envelope*) Yes, sir.

FREED goes out, already interested in the wording on the envelope.

MANN:	(*To QUINTON*) So you know about the cable to Genoa?
QUINTON:	(*After a moment*) Yes, Inspector.
MANN:	(*A suggestion of irritation*) You knew about it before Ryder told his story?
QUINTON:	(*Nodding*) There was a copy on my desk an hour after it was sent.
MANN:	(*Looking at SMITH, then back to QUINTON*) Mr Quinton, don't you think you owe me an explanation?
QUINTON:	Yes, Inspector – and a drink.

QUINTON crosses to the desk and opens a concealed cupboard in front of the desk; there are several bottles, decanters, glasses, etc in the cupboard.

QUINTON: (*To SMITH, as he gets out the required glasses etc*) Go on, George.

SMITH comes from behind the desk and sits on the arm of a chair, facing MANN.

SMITH: Geoffrey Ryder told you an interesting story this afternoon. Part of that story was true and part of it, pure invention. But forget Ryder's story for the moment, because I want to tell you about Dr Charles Elroyd. Many years ago, Elroyd was a member of a certain political group; after a time, he broke away from the group and became, to use his own words, bleakly disinterested in politics.

QUINTON: (*To the INSPECTOR, as he mixes one of the drinks*) We're not telling you anything about Elroyd that he wouldn't tell you himself. The man's perfectly frank.

SMITH: (*Nodding*) Twelve months ago, Elroyd was introduced to David Weldon. Weldon's a curious character and something of a dilettante.

QUINTON: As a matter of fact, Ryder gave us a very good description of him.

SMITH: It soon became apparent to Elroyd that Weldon's interest in him was not entirely due to the fact that he played a good game of bridge. Elroyd became suspicious, so much so, in fact, that he consulted Mr Quinton.

QUINTON: As a result of this we made certain inquiries and discovered that Weldon had entertained quite a number of people at his home in Mount Street.

SMITH: Including two well known diplomats, who are no longer with us, and a certain Nuclear Physicist.

QUINTON: In short, David Weldon was the gentleman we'd been looking for ever since the Burg incident – since 1949.

MANN: Go on, sir.

QUINTON: Weldon eventually put a proposition to Elroyd and acting on our instructions the doctor accepted it. He was due to leave for Rome on October 8th; about ten days before this however Weldon introduced him to Geoffrey Ryder.

MANN: But Ryder said …

QUINTON: (*Smiling*) Whatever Ryder may have said, Inspector, he came here for the express purpose of accompanying Dr Elroyd to Italy. His instructions were to keep the doctor under close observation until he was handed over to a Special Agent at Tolero – that's about twenty minutes from Rome.

MANN: (*To QUINTON*) Go on, sir.

QUINTON gives the INSPECTOR one of the drinks.

QUINTON: We intended to let them get as far as Dover and then pick up Ryder. But there were two unexpected developments. One: Ryder became suspicious. Two: he went down with malaria.

MANN: And David Weldon?

QUINTON: When Weldon heard that Ryder was in hospital, he became frightened; obviously realising, of course, that Ryder might become delirious and talk.

103

SMITH:	Consequently, we haven't seen or heard anything of Mr Weldon from that day to this.
MANN:	And Dr Elroyd?
QUINTON:	(*After a moment*) We felt that we'd taken enough chances with Dr Elroyd. He's in Canada.
MANN:	I see.

There is a knock on the door and FREED enters. He carries the envelope and a separate sheet of notepaper. He hands both the envelope and the notepaper to QUINTON. SMITH crosses and takes one of the drinks which QUINTON has mixed.

QUINTON:	(*Studying the notepaper*) Good work, Freed.
FREED:	(*Faintly surprised*) Thank you, sir.
QUINTON:	(*Offering MANN the notepaper*) That's what the advertisement really meant, Inspector.

The INSPECTOR takes the sheet of notepaper and looks at it. We see the message reads:

"Imperative you see me immediately. I shall be at the Knightsbridge flat every afternoon. Walter Smedley".

MANN:	Well, that's pretty clear. But how does Smedley fit into all this? Did Ryder really meet him in Paris?

QUINTON crosses to the desk and opens one of the drawers.

SMITH:	He met him all right, but a very different Smedley from the one he described. It was Smedley that put the Elroyd proposition to him.
QUINTON:	(*Taking a notebook out of the desk and opening it*) You remember the cable that Ryder sent as soon as he arrived at the flat?
MANN:	About the cigarette case?
QUINTON:	It was in code. (*He reads from the notebook*) "Am prepared to go ahead, but have not yet

	heard from your agent, please tell him to contact me."
MANN:	Meaning David Weldon?
SMITH:	Exactly.
MANN:	Then all that business about Smedley's cigarette case?
QUINTON:	Was pure invention to cover up the reference in the cable.
MANN:	But we found a cigarette case by Smedley's body.
QUINTON:	Of course you did. Ryder saw to that all right – it strengthened his story.
MANN:	But why was the Sleeper reserved in Smedley's name when presumably it was intended for Ryder?
QUINTON:	Because the Sleeper was booked by Smedley before Ryder accepted the proposition.
SMITH:	The fact that the Sleeper was in Smedley's name didn't mean a thing; obviously whoever produced the ticket occupied the Sleeper.
MANN:	I see. And Katherine Weldon?
SMITH:	She doesn't exist. Ryder invented her to strengthen his story about Smedley and to justify both his association with Weldon and the reference in the cable.
QUINTON:	You see, if you really stop to think about it, Ryder's story was pretty ingenious. It gave innocent explanations to a series of incriminating incidents. It explains what he was doing in London, how he met Weldon, and why he became friendly with Elroyd. It also completely justified his cable to Genoa.
SMITH:	In order to strengthen his story, he even threw suspicion on to Elroyd.

105

MANN:	But why did he insist on making a statement to you, Mr Quinton, instead of to Scotland Yard?
QUINTON:	Because he knew that if he didn't clear himself so far as we were concerned, he hadn't a very good chance of escaping the murder charge.
SMITH:	Ryder covered himself on every point and when he couldn't cover himself – as in the case of the photographs – he deliberately confused the issue.
QUINTON:	He obviously intended to tell you about the photographs and then changed his mind and produced the flag.
MANN:	It was his own flag of course, the one he brought over with him.
QUINTON:	(*Nodding*) Yes. It's difficult to say why he changed his mind.
SMITH:	If you ask me, he suddenly realised he was out of his depth.
QUINTON:	You may be right, George.
MANN:	I suppose there's no doubt that Ryder did murder Smedley?
QUINTON:	No doubt. You'll realise that when you've heard the recording.
MANN:	Recording?
SMITH:	We installed a recorder in the flat while Ryder was in hospital. We have a record of his conversation with Smedley.
QUINTON:	Would you like to hear it, Inspector?
MANN:	(*With a note of sarcasm*) Well, it might be worth my while, sir.

QUINTON: (*A suggestion of a smile*) I'm afraid our methods may seem a little unorthodox – but at times we deal with rather unorthodox people.

MANN: Yes, – but don't lose sight of the fact that so far as we're concerned this is a murder case!

The telephone rings and FREED crosses to the desk and picks up the receiver.

FREED: (*On the telephone*) Hello …

Crosscut to a telephone box in Knightsbridge. SERGEANT GORRINGE is in the box holding the receiver.

GORRINGE: (*On the other end*) Is that Mr Quinton's office?

FREED: Yes …

GORRINGE: I want to speak to Inspector Mann – this is Detective Sergeant Gorringe.

FREED: Just a moment.

The INSPECTOR takes the receiver off FREED.

MANN: Yes – what is it, Sergeant?

GORRINGE: The flat's empty, sir. He left an hour ago.

MANN: Are you sure?

GORRINGE: Yes, one of the tradespeople saw him. Something must have scared him, sir – apparently he was in a devil of a hurry.

MANN: Yes, all right, Sergeant.

MANN replaces the receiver.

QUINTON: What is it?

MANN: (*To QUINTON*) Ryder's gone – he's made a dash for it.

SMITH: (*To MANN*) He obviously didn't think you believed his story.

MANN: (*Shaking his head; annoyed*) That's not the reason. (*He looks at QUINTON*) Is that recording contraption of yours still in the flat?

QUINTON: Yes.

MANN:	(*Angrily*) Well, it's my bet he found it!
QUINTON:	(*Looks at SMITH, then nods*) I think he's right.
MANN:	Apparently unorthodox methods don't always pay, Mr Quinton! (*Turning towards the door*) Well, whatever happened we've got to find Ryder!
FREED:	(*Quietly*) I should advertise for him, Inspector.
MANN:	(*Turning; astonished*) What did you say?
FREED:	I said: I should advertise for him.
MANN:	(*Angrily*) Are you trying to be funny?
QUINTON:	(*Suddenly*) Wait a minute! (*He moves across to FREED, stands staring at him for a moment; he looks thoughtful, serious*) I think you've got something there …

CUT TO: *A glass showcase outside of a small newsagents-cum-tobacconists. The case contains numerous typed, printed, and handwritten postcards advertising various goods for sale or part exchanges; also advertisements for Daily Help; Articles Lost and Found; Pets for sale; etc. etc.*
The camera tracks in on a postcard which reads:
"Gentleman wishes to sell or exchange gold cigarette case. Interested in good second-hand typewriter or television set. Please ring Western 3127 before 8 o'clock."
The camera holds tight on the card and then superimposes a second card identical in make-up. (This is the first card decoded: seen through the eyes of GEOFFREY RYDER.) It reads:
"New situation has arisen re – Elroyd. Will personally pay you the five hundred. Meet me Knightsbridge flat eight o'clock, Thursday evening, Weldon."
Superimpose back to the original card.

CUT TO: The Flat. The Living Room. 8 o'clock Thursday evening.

The lights are on, and the curtains are drawn. QUINTON is stubbing out a cigarette in a large glass ashtray; there are one or two cigarette ends already in the ashtray. INSPECTOR MANN is sitting on the arm of a chair watching the entrance into the hall. After a moment he turns towards QUINTON.

MANN: What time is it?

QUINTON: (*Glancing at his watch*) Nearly a quarter past eight …

MANN: (*Shaking his head*) He's not coming …

QUINTON: (*Calmly*) There's still plenty of time …

MANN: (*Faintly on edge*) No, no, it's my bet he's not coming.

QUINTON: It's my bet he's still making up his mind. (*Looking at MANN; friendly*) Are you in a hurry, Inspector?

MANN: (*Surprised*) Me? Why, no, sir.

QUINTON: (*Smiling*) Relax …

MANN doesn't know whether to be offended by QUINTON's remark or not; suddenly he smiles.

MANN: I'm not used to this sort of thing, sir. At heart I'm just a terrific cop.

QUINTON: At heart I am an archaeologist.

MANN: You, sir?

QUINTON: Yes.

MANN: Is that what you did before you were with M.I.5.?

QUINTON nods.

MANN: Why did you give it up?

QUINTON: It gave me up.

MANN: (*After a moment*) Where's your colleague tonight?

109

QUINTON: George? He's at London Airport; he's leaving for Nice.

MANN: You people get about.

QUINTON: Yes ... (*A moment; amused*) I'll bet he's as nervous as a kitten.

MANN: Why – doesn't he like flying?

QUINTON: He likes flying all right, but he's going on holiday.

MANN: Why should that make him nervous?

QUINTON: In 1951, he went to Switzerland, and got caught in an avalanche; the following year he went to France, in time for the French Railway strike; in '52 he went to Greece ...

MANN: The earthquake?

QUINTON: Yes.

MANN: And what happened last year?

QUINTON: He played safe and went to Paignton. The hotel caught fire.

The INSPECTOR laughs, and as he does so the telephone starts to ring. MANN stops laughing and looks across to QUINTON who rises; he stares down at the telephone.

MANN: (*Tensely*) That's Ryder – he's checking up to see if Weldon's here.

QUINTON: (*Angrily; softly*) The damn fools! I told the Exchange to report this number out of order.

They stand by the table; the telephone continues to ring. After a long pause, and with almost a gesture of defiance, QUINTON snatches up the receiver. He holds it in his hand, not yet to his ear.

OPERATOR's VOICE: (*On the other end*) Hello? ... Hello ... Mr Quinton ... Mr Quinton ... Hello? ...

QUINTON slowly puts the receiver to his ear.

OPERATOR's VOICE: (*On the other end; much clearer*) Mr Quinton?

QUINTON: Yes …

OPERATOR's VOICE: This is the Supervisor, sir. I'm sorry, I know we've had orders to report this number out of order but there's a Colonel Smith on the line. He says it's urgent …

QUINTON: Put him through …

MANN: (*To QUINTON; puzzled*) Who is it?

QUINTON: It's George!

MANN: (*Quickly*) I thought you said he was at the Airport?

There is a click on the line.

SMITH: (*On the other end of the line; tense and excited*) Alan, this is George!

QUINTON: What is it, George?

SMITH: Listen – I've seen Weldon!

QUINTON: (*Staggered*) What?

SMITH is in a telephone box at London Airport and from now on we crosscut between him and QUINTON.

SMITH: He's here, at the Airport – he's leaving for Zurich on the 8.15 plane.

QUINTON: Are you sure?

SMITH: Of course I'm sure!

QUINTON: (*Tensely; hardly able to control his excitement*) Now, listen, George! Don't let him catch that plane …

SMITH: How the hell can I stop him? I haven't got a warrant! I daren't even question him!

QUINTON: (*Shouting*) George, I don't care what you do – or how you do it – break every rule in the book – but stop him!

SMITH: (*He hesitates and looks at the receiver*) Right!

SMITH replaces the receiver.

CUT TO: The Flat. The Living Room.
QUINTON's hand is stubbing out another cigarette in the ashtray which is now full of cigarette ends. He is sitting at the table playing Patience. The INSPECTOR is still sitting on the arm of the chair; he looks worried and tired. MANN rises and crosses to QUINTON; he stands looking down at the cards.

QUINTON: (*Not looking up*) We'll give him another half an hour.

MANN: Yes, all right.

A pause.

QUINTON: (*Indicating the cards*) You know, I could never understand that game. No head for cards. Freed's the one …

MANN: I'll bet he is. (*Suddenly; tensely*) I wonder how he made out?

QUINTON: (*Looking up; smiling; he knows full well what the INSPECTOR means*) Freed?

MANN: No, no, your friend Smith.

QUINTON: Don't worry about George – he'd think of something.

MANN: It's to be hoped so! My God, if you lose Weldon and we lose Ryder …

QUINTON: Sit down, Inspector – have another cigarette.

MANN looks at QUINTON, is about to say something and then changes his mind. He crosses the room, stares at the picture on the wall, turns and then casually picks up a book. He flicks the pages, then suddenly stops dead: he looks across at QUINTON. QUINTON is about to play a card; he hesitates; looks across at the INSPECTOR. He slowly puts down the card and rises. The INSPECTOR puts down the book and turns towards the hall.

CUT TO: The Flat. The Hall.

GEOFFREY is slowly, cautiously, entering the flat. He closes the door behind him, but deliberately doesn't latch it. He looks at the hall table which has a bowler hat and a pair of gloves on it. GEOFFREY crosses the hall towards the living room door.

CUT TO: The Flat. The Living Room.

The INSPECTOR and QUINTON are waiting for GEOFFREY. He enters and stops dead at the sight of MANN and QUINTON.

MANN: Good evening, Mr Ryder!

GEOFFREY: (*Tensely*) Where's Weldon?

QUINTON: Well, we hope he's been unavoidably detained. However, I gather you got the message all right.

GEOFFREY suddenly turns and rushes back into the hall.

CUT TO: The Flat. The Hall.

The door has been pushed open and GEORGE SMITH, complete with two suitcases and a zip bag, stands in the open doorway. GEOFFREY stops dead, takes a revolver from his pocket, and turning fires into the living room. Almost simultaneous with the shot we hear QUINTON's voice "Look out" and the smashing of glass. SMITH realises what is happening and immediately drops the suitcases and throws the zip bag straight at GEOFFREY. It hits him full-on and he drops the revolver. He stoops to try to revolver it. As he does so a man's foot appears and steps on the revolver. Almost simultaneously there is the sound of a blow. GEOFFREY falls spark out on the floor with QUINTON standing over him. MANN kneels beside GEOFFREY; he looks up at QUINTON and smiles.

MANN: That was one hell of a wallop for an archaeologist!

SMITH joins QUINTON and MANN.

QUINTON: (*Quickly; turning on SMITH*) What happened, George?

SMITH: I hit him with the jolly old zipper.

QUINTON: No, no, no, at the Airport!

SMITH: Oh, I missed the plane, old boy.

QUINTON: George, what happened?

SMITH: I missed the plane. Had to pick up a cab. I shall put this lark on my expense account.

QUINTON: (*Desperately*) George, what happened to Weldon?

SMITH: Oh, Weldon! (*He smiles*) Don't worry about Weldon, he's been taken care of.

MANN: Did our people pick him up?

SMITH: Yes – he was just getting on the plane. I say, what a diabolical character. Do you know what he did?

QUINTON: No?

SMITH: He pinched my wallet.

QUINTON: Pinched your wallet?

SMITH: Yes, I had to kick up a devil of a stink. Anyway, they found it on him all right.

MANN and QUINTON are amused.

QUINTON: Nice work, George.

SMITH: (*Pulling the lobe of his ear; thoughtful*) I'm a bit worried.

QUINTON: Why?

SMITH: Well, apparently, they're holding him on a currency charge.

QUINTON: A currency charge!

SMITH: Yes. There was fifty quid in the wallet.

QUINTON gives SMITH a look.

SMITH: (*With a nervous little smile*) You said – break every rule in the book, old boy.

CUT TO: A First-Class Railway Carriage.

The carriage is empty, then QUINTON enters and takes a seat. He wears a bowler hat and carries a rolled umbrella. He puts the umbrella on the rack and settles down for a quiet doze. There is the noise of the door opening and closing and MR HENSON enters. He is a middle-aged man; very sure of himself; a grumbler; he carries an evening paper. He sits next to QUINTON.

HENSON: By George, I've only just made it!

QUINTON opens an eye, glances at HENSON, then prepares to doze.

HENSON: Not a very nice night.

QUINTON ignores him. HENSON opens his paper and prepares to read.

A pause.

HENSON: I see there's no news about this chap Elroyd.

QUINTON: (*Opening his eyes*) I beg your pardon?

HENSON: (*Indicating his paper*) I said: there's no news about this chap Elroyd.

QUINTON: (*Vaguely*) Oh – no …

HENSON: (*Shaking his head*) I don't know, I'm sure. It takes a bit of weighing up. Fancy letting a chap like that get away …

QUINTON: (*Sleepily*) I beg your pardon?

HENSON: I said fancy letting a … (*Amazed*) Haven't you read about this? He's one of our top scientists. He's scarpered.

QUINTON: Scarpered?

HENSON: Vamoosed. It's damn serious.

QUINTON: Yes, I suppose it is.

HENSON:	I mean, it's just not good enough. This sort of thing isn't going to get us anywhere. We've got to change our ideas, old man – pull our socks up.
QUINTON:	(*Vaguely*) Yes, I suppose we have.
HENSON:	Documents disappearing, scientists scarpering, diplomats …
QUINTON:	(*Politely*) Vamoosing?
HENSON:	Exactly! (*A moment then he leans forward towards QUINTON*) I've got a friend who's got a cousin who's got a brother with M.I.5. (*Confidentially*) Dead from the neck up.
QUINTON:	(*Politely*) Your friend's cousin?
HENSON:	No, no, no, M.I.5.
QUINTON:	Really?
HENSON:	(*Pleased with himself*) That surprises you, doesn't it?
QUINTON:	Faintly …
HENSON:	(*Very confidential*) Half the Secret Service, old boy … (*He makes a drinking gesture with his right hand*)
QUINTON:	No!
HENSON:	(*Emphatically, slowly nodding his head*) Yes! (*He opens his paper; he has impressed himself*) If you knew half the things that went on, you'd be amazed – amazed.
QUINTON:	(*Certainly a thought*) Yes, I suppose I would.

There is a pause.

QUINTON sits back; after a moment he dozes.

HANSON reads his paper, he is not at all impressed by what he reads.

HENSON:	(*Shaking his head with disapproval*) T't – T't – T't. They're sleeping on the job. Just sleeping on the job.

The camera tracks in on QUINTON sleeping.

THE END

Names, titles and places in Francis Durbridge

by Dr Georg Pagitz, leading expert on Francis Durbridge

Francis Durbridge was a perfectionist. This can be seen in many aspects of his work, for example in the plots, which are sophisticated down to the smallest detail, in the sophisticated cliffhangers and twists and, last but not least, in the choice of names for his characters and in the titles for his works.

Regarding this the author has left nothing to chance. If one takes a closer look at his *oeuvre*, you will notice that the names of the characters could hardly have been more appropriately chosen. That's why Francis Durbridge kept a small notebook in which he wrote down names and titles that he liked. When he started a new work, he referred to it. Within his own family, he revealed little about the current plots, but often sounded them out about what they thought about one name or another.

Throughout Francis Durbridge's entire creative period, it can be observed how often he reconsidered and changed the names and titles of his works. This manifests itself not only when his scripts have been translated into other languages and the characters have had to be renamed for secrecy reasons, but also in different stages of some works.

This is already evident in his first big success: The novelist who solves criminal cases was originally supposed to be called Mark Conway. Durbridge then dropped this name in favour of Paul Temple, but later used it in 1940 and 1941 in other radio productions that did not feature Temple. Durbridge must have liked the name Mark very much, because he later used it frequently for his characters, including the protagonist of his first television serial *The Broken Horseshoe* (1952), who appears again in *Operation Diplomat* (1952). By the way, the difficulty in choosing the

119

name of the main character later also becomes apparent with his second very well-known investigator, namely Tim Frazer. He was originally supposed to be called David Marquand. The name Mark appears phonetically here as it did also with one of Paul Temple's villains The Marquis. Needless to say, both Marquand and Frazer (albeit in other spellings) appeared in many other works.

The fact that Francis Durbridge liked the names of his sons Stephen and Nicholas is also shown by the fact that he uses these two first names particularly often in his works, not only for characters, but also for places and houses: St. Stephen or St. Nic(h)olas. The name Stephen also appears abbreviated in 'Steve' and it is certainly no coincidence that Durbridge chose the pseudonym Nicholas (Vane) for some of his works. The climax of this is most apparent in the story of *Lightfingers*, in which Paul Temple is invited by a certain Sir Stephen, who lives in Nicholas Hall. It is all the more interesting that his own first name Francis and that of his wife Norah never appear in his stories.

Whether a character is good or evil can often be recognized quite quickly by the name given them by Durbridge. In almost all of his stories, there is the character who is an informant from the underworld or that of the ice-cold henchman who carries out the orders of the great unknown. These characters never have normal names. Whoever was called Snipey Jackson, Lefty Rogers, Snow Williams or Clutch Brompton usually had a criminal record – some of whom were now trying to go straight and who usually did not survive the story.

It is well known that Edgar Wallace was a great role model for Francis Durbridge. His first work, *Send for Paul Temple* (1938), contains a lot of elements typical of Wallace's work. So it is not surprising that Durbridge names two of his characters after main characters from the two most famous works of Edgar Wallace: Milton was the protagonist in *The Ringer*, Trent (the professional name of Steve) was the surname of the female main character in *The Squeaker*. Other allusions to Edgar Wallace are undoubtedly the existence of a mysterious room 7 (in Wallace's case it was room 13) and the naming of the mastermind behind it with Knave of Diamonds, after all, there was a Wallace novel in which a Knave of Clubs played a similar role (*Jack O'Judgement*). The homage to the King of Crime are nowhere as strong as in Durbridge's first work, but he also repeats this appreciation again and again later, for example when he gives one of his television serials the title *The Desperate People* which is reminiscent Wallace's *The Terrible People* or when he gives one of characters the name of Gordon Stewart in the German version of *Bat out of Hell*, *Wie ein Blitz* (1970), a name that sounds identical to Gordon Stuart, a character from the well-known Wallace novel *The Dark Eyes of London*.

We see this again when Francis Durbridge writes *A Man Called Harry Brent*. Here he calls the detective Milton, like the main character from Wallace's *The Ringer*. When he revised the script for the German market and renamed the characters, he changed Inspector Milton to become Inspector Wallace thus giving him the name of the author he so much admired.

It is also interesting to note that many characters were given surnames of other famous writers: so there are numerous Hemingways (like Ernest), Zolas (like Émile) and Wallaces (like Edgar) in the different stories. The surname of John O'Hara, another author admired by Durbridge, also appears several times. Collins is a fairly common name, but Francis Durbridge certainly knew of Wilkie Collins' well-known work *The Woman in White*, which laid the foundation for modern crime fiction. It is certainly no coincidence that in *Tim Frazer and the Salinger Affair*, two characters are called

Fairlie and Gilmore, who are characters in Collins' masterpiece.

Durbridge loved to travel, so it's no wonder he used names for his characters from his trips to the continent. This is what happened, for example, with the character Dr. Linderhof in *The Desperate People* (1963), which he certainly named after the Bavarian castle of the same name, which he had visited with his family in the early 1960s.

Another name, Timothy, is very much associated with Durbridge. Today, one can't say how and why the author came up with this name. It was certainly used because in the 1930s you couldn't use swear words or curses so Temple is often heard to exclaim "By Timothy!" instead of some blasphemous. Durbridge also shortens the name Timothy to Tim for his popular tv hero – Tim Frazer and for the main character Tim Forrester in the tv serial *Portrait of Alison*. It is also interesting – and this is just a side note – that Timothy was also brought to life. So Steve is pregnant at the end of *Send for Paul Temple Again!* (1945) their child – a boy – appears in *A Case for Paul Temple* (1946) when we learn that he is with the nanny at Bramley Lodge. In *Paul Temple and the Curzon Case* (1948) we learn the name of Temple's son is Timothy, but this is the last we hear of him for we never learn what became of young Timothy Temple.

Anyone who examines the different stages of Francis Durbridge's works will see that he used and re-used the same basic plot ideas but changed the characters names when he saw fit throughout his life. For example, he followed *Send for Paul Temple* (1938) with the novel *Beware of Johnny Washington* (1951), the same plot but with different character names, which was followed by an almost identical text called *One Man to Another*, which differed from Johnny Washington only in the character names.

In addition to the names, the choice of title was also essential. For example, the name Durbridge's famous play *Suddenly at Home* came to him when he read it in a death obituary notice. The title *Bat Out of Hell*, on the other hand, is said to go back to a comment made by a director who when asked by Durbridge how the shooting of his new film went replied "It went like a bat out of hell."

The extent to which ideas were returned to can also be seen in the play *Z.4*: This is what Durbridge called the criminal organization in the third Paul Temple adventure *News of Paul Temple* (1939). Many years later, in the 1980s, he wrote a play based on a 1946 radio play, *The Caspary Affair*, which premiered in the UK in 1993 as *Sweet Revenge*. A heart medication called Zarabell 4 (abbreviated Z.4!) plays a decisive role in it. An earlier version of the play was performed in Germany in 1988. Of course with different character names, but also the medication had a different name: Zaradin 4! This was also the German and Durbridge's working title. This is just another example of how much the author honed every detail of his work, often over years and decades.